MR014

THE PROMISE REMAINS

THE
Promise
REMAINS

A Novella by
TRAVIS THRASHER

Tyndale House Publishers, Inc.
WHEATON, ILLINOIS

To the sweet and adorable girl
who asked me to be her partner in our high school play
and who has remained by my side ever since.
I love you, Sharon.

ACKNOWLEDGMENTS

With special thanks:

To my parents, for loving and encouraging me.

To my sister, for putting up with me.

To Ron Beers, for seeing so much potential not only in a novel but also in a crazy kid he hired.

To Anne Goldsmith, for your honesty and encouragement regarding my writing career.

To Anne Christian Buchanan, for making this story as good as it could be.

To Francine Rivers, for telling me to write the story in my heart.

To Jerry Jenkins, for your insight, encouragement, and friendship.

To Catherine Palmer, for never once doubting this would happen.

To the Macks, Odells, Pehrsons, and Swobodas, for your loving prayers.

And finally, to anyone anywhere who ever listened to my dreams from third grade on—well, you're holding one of them in your hands.

Love never gives up,
never loses faith, is always hopeful,
and endures through every circumstance.
1 Corinthians 13:7

prologue

THE YOUNG WOMAN stood on the deck of the log cabin, looking into the tear-filled eyes of the man she loved. The normal mixture of mischievous charm and boyish confidence was gone. In its place lay emptiness and defeat.

All because of her.

The pain in his face caused an answering wrench in her heart. Yet she still couldn't utter a single word in response to his question.

He countered her silence by asking again, this time with more urgency, "Will you marry me?"

Words she had waited a lifetime to hear. A question she had prayed would one day come.

Another suffocating moment passed. Finally, she gasped her answer. "I can't."

With the simple utterance of two seemingly insignificant words, all the hope and longing held in her heart vanished. The memories forged by years of dreams meant nothing now. Just like that, it was over.

Snow began to fall, reminding her of where she was.

I can't believe I'm doing this, she thought. *Dear Father, please forgive me for hurting him. You know I don't want to hurt him.*

"There has to be a way," he said. "I don't understand."

"No—"

"I'll give you time to think. Maybe all you need is time."

"I've had time," she replied. "I'm sorry."

"This can't be happening," he said. "Not like this. Not now."

She stopped herself from apologizing again. "I don't know what else to say."

"Say anything except no. Say there's a chance. There has to be, right? Say something. Give me some bit of hope."

"I don't know."

He choked her name out. "There has to be a chance. All these years. You know how I feel, and I know—at least I thought I knew—how you feel."

"You do," she said, afraid of what he would say next.

"Then why? Why are you doing this?"

"I've explained it to you."

"There has to be another reason. Something that makes better sense. Tell me you don't like my sense of humor. Or the way I dress. Or something like that. Give me something that makes sense."

"I just—" And then came her tears.

"Oh, man, I'm sorry," he said, his hands cupping hers. "I didn't mean to say all that. I'm sorry. Please, don't look away."

When she glanced up again, she marveled that his smile looked as warm now as it had when she first met him. Even years later, she could still remember it—the carefree and engaging grin that had captivated her. The smile that could still appear anytime she closed her eyes in the midst of life's little problems.

But this was not one of life's little problems; this was her whole life. Her whole life shattering before her very eyes.

"I'm sorry," he said again. "I shouldn't go on like this—I'm just making it harder for you. I do respect your convictions—that's one of the reasons I love you so much. I just don't know how to . . . well, I know this sounds corny, but I don't know how to let you go."

Her tears began to fall faster now, and she knew she was losing control. She didn't want to cry—not this way, not if they were saying their final goodbyes.

"I'm trying to think of something more to say than sorry," she said.

"You don't have to. I just want to hold you and tell you I love you."

How can you? she asked herself. *How can you say those things after what I'm doing to you?*

As she embraced him, she searched for the right thing to say. There were so many words she wanted to utter, so much of her soul she needed to bare. But the words failed her.

"I'm never going to stop loving you," he whispered in her ear. "I promise you with everything I have and everything I am that my love for you will never die."

How can you say that? her mind screamed. *How can you even dare make such a promise?*

She knew if she didn't leave soon, her resolve would weaken. She would retract her words and reaffirm her undying love, only to resume the battle of heart and mind that had brought her to this point in the first place.

"I have to go," she said, pulling away from him. "The storm—"

"I know."

She took a few steps away from him, then turned. "I'm going to make a promise to you, too," she declared. "I'm never giving up on you. Every night I'm going to pray that you find your place in this world, that you find hope."

"I've already found my place," he replied, wiping his eyes. "It's by your side."

I know, she thought as she carefully stepped down the snowcapped steps leading off the deck. *God, why does this have to feel so wrong—when I know I'm doing the right thing?*

The word *promise* seemed to echo off the surrounding snowbanks.

"Don't forget this," he called out behind her. She turned again. He was following her down the steps, holding out something in his hand.

"No, I can't. Seriously . . ."

"Please take it," he said as he wrapped her hand around the small case. "I don't want it. It's yours. You're the only one it can ever belong to."

She walked toward her car, urging her feet and her heart not to turn back. Her fingers still clutched the little box she just couldn't open. She knew it held a ring.

Will I ever be able to look at it? God, will you ever give me the chance to?

"Don't forget me," his voice rose over the howling winds.

With a turbulent heart that mirrored the approaching storm, she believed they would be the last words she would ever hear him say.

PART 1

USA

Where can I begin?

secrets

SARA ANTHONY opened her eyes and wondered where she was. After glancing around the room for a few minutes, she saw a card propped open on the nightstand next to her and then remembered.

It's been a long time since I woke up in my old bed.

Actually, it had been exactly a year since she had last spent the night at her parents' house. Exactly a year since she had taken her mother's suggestion of sleeping over, even though her town home was only twenty minutes away. Mom had asked her again this year, and Sara had found no reason to refuse. In fact, she enjoyed this new tradition of spending the night before her birthday with her parents.

Her birthday. . . *Can I really be thirty years old?* she asked herself. *I don't feel like I'm thirty.*

The date told her otherwise: June 11. Sara rubbed her 8:30 A.M. eyes and read the card.

> *To Our Beloved Daughter.*
> *No matter how old you are,*
> *you'll always be our little girl.*
> *Happy Birthday.*

Her mother had signed the bottom of the card.

"Sara: We are so proud of you. You are such a blessing to both of us. We love you. Mom and Dad"

Carrying the card, Sara padded sleepily downstairs, where the scent of Mom's breakfast and Dad's coffee greeted her. Before even asking she knew the flavors of the day: blueberry pancakes, her favorite, and hazelnut-blend coffee. Birthday-morning pancakes and coffee were an Anthony household tradition.

"It's the birthday girl." Her dad sat at the table, smiling over the sports pages of the *Atlanta Constitution*.

"Happy birthday, dear," her mom added, following her greeting with a hug.

"Thanks. And thanks for the card. But I've got to tell you—I'm still in denial about this birthday stuff. So I'm going to try to enjoy some of this beautiful day without being depressed."

Sara poured herself a cup of coffee—she owed her caffeine habit to her father—and sat down at the table.

"There is nothing depressing about having a birthday," Mom stated in her firmest, most optimistic voice.

"Unless you're turning thirty," Sara said, a bit of sharpness in her morning voice.

"What's wrong with thirty?" her father asked.

"Nothing if you're married and have a family. But for us single ladies—"

"Who's single?"

She looked at her dad and smiled. "Okay, not single. But unmarried. Not that I'm rushing to get married or anything, but still . . ."

"Your time will come."

"I know. It probably will. But I always thought I'd have a family by thirty. It was one of those unspoken goals."

"I always wanted to climb Mt. Everest by the time I was thirty."

"I didn't know you were a climber," Sara said to her father.

"Well, I'm not. But you know, that was one of my unspoken goals. Just because you have them doesn't mean you actually have to fulfill them."

Sara glanced at her mother and was surprised at her silence. Sara's unmarried state was one of Lila Anthony's favorite topics of speculation. But maybe she was deliberately biting her tongue in honor of the day, Sara reflected gratefully.

"Breakfast smells great, Mom."

"It's your favorite—blueberry pancakes. Your father has been nagging me to make them for several weeks now."

"I have not," he said, winking at Sara. "I'm fully content with my usual bagel every morning."

Sara leaned back in her chair and sipped her coffee.

"I'm really tired this morning," she told her parents. "I don't know why."

"You're an old lady now," her father said with a laugh.

"What time did you go to bed last night?" Mom asked in a statement that really meant *What time did Bruce leave?*

"About eleven or so," Sara replied. She did not explain further.

"How's Bruce doing?"

"Good, as always. We just went to a movie." Sara proceeded to describe the film, carefully avoiding any further mention of Bruce, dating, marriage, family . . . or any other subject her mother might pounce on.

Being the only child had many benefits, Sara realized, but sometimes she wished she had a younger brother or sister. Then maybe she wouldn't be so pampered, so cared about, so *scrutinized*. She loved her parents and felt a close bond with each of them. Yet sometimes they still treated her like a little girl instead of a twenty-nine-year-old woman.

Make that thirty-year-old, she thought with a sick feeling. *Thirty years old, and I'm still here being babied and questioned.* She thought of the birthday card: *You'll always be our little girl.*

She sighed. But then she looked over at the large stacks of delicious pancakes and told herself she really couldn't complain.

Her mother served the pancakes, starting off with the stack that held the lit candle.

"Mom," Sara said, rolling her eyes. "Please." But she had to smile.

"Now we all have to sing."

And as the three of them sang the corny tune of "Happy Birthday," Sara felt her morning mood lift. She found herself thanking God—not only for having another birthday, but for having such loving parents.

Sara shifted to fifth gear as she accelerated five miles above the speed limit on the highway connecting her parents' neighborhood of Groveton, Georgia, to her town home in Rex. The white Toyota convertible she drove was her birthday present—a present from her parents, who had helped on the down payment—and from herself. It had only two hundred and twenty miles on it so far, and the new-car smell from the leather seats filled her with delight. It was the first brand-new car she had ever owned—an unaccustomed luxury. Sara hardly ever bought herself anything except the basic necessities and an occasional outfit for school. But outfits that would become stained with paint and chocolate and markers as she taught kindergarten were necessities, too. The car was a bit extravagant, but she figured she would only turn thirty once. Besides, she was thinking that it was time she made some changes in her life. She had been in a holding pattern way too long.

Wind whipped her long bangs across her sunglasses. She listened to a combination of her favorite CDs as she drove past kudzu-covered walls edging the freeway. The Atlanta skyline could be seen in the distance on her left, but today she ignored it entirely. Something about the clear and beautiful summer day made her unaccountably sad.

Sara had lived in the town of Rex since moving into her town home five years ago. She liked having a place she could call her own while still being close enough to visit her parents. She enjoyed her job as a kindergarten teacher at a public grade school only minutes away from home. She also loved the summertime break, when she became more involved with ministries in her church and with the friends in her small group.

Her father, Daniel Anthony, managed the computer technical-services division at a business in downtown Atlanta. He had worked there ever since the move to Georgia during Sara's college years.

The move. The dreaded move. They had lived at the end of Herrington Lane in Groveton for the last ten years. The move from the small town of Maryville, Tennessee, had taken place just before Sara's twentieth birthday. Even after ten years, Sara still did not consider Georgia her home. Home would always be where she had left a part of her heart. She understood the opportunity the job had offered her father and their family, but the memories of the Smoky Mountains still brought an ache deep inside her, reminding her of a monumental loss in her life.

A loss her parents would never know about.

Sara thought about her mother and dad. She knew they looked forward to the one day she would walk down the aisle and say "I do" to the man of her dreams. Why wouldn't they eagerly await that moment? Sara certainly did.

I never thought I'd wake up alone on the day I turned thirty.

9 ≈ secrets

Sara knew that her sociable, energetic mother was disappointed that her one and only child was still unwed. Lila was one of those dynamic, take-charge women who liked to do things right, and Sara's unmarried state seemed to make her mother feel strangely incomplete. Besides, Lila positively salivated at the prospect of planning a big, beautiful wedding, and she couldn't wait for grand-children. She had talked more and more about marriage as time passed—especially since Bruce had come on the scene.

But Sara found herself hesitant to think about the M-word. Yes, she did want to get married, but she didn't feel as ready as her mother wanted her to be. And yes, she cared deeply for her boy-friend, Bruce Erickson. But marriage was such a big step. Such an incredible commitment. One Sara had not wanted to face the last couple of years.

In her mother's eyes, Sara and Bruce were more than ready. Sara knew her mother was already collecting brides' magazines and browsing in wedding shops.

Could she ever be like her mother? The two of them certainly looked alike—both small and dark—but her mother carried an air of sophistication and confidence Sara knew she could never carry off. Everything about Lila Anthony was organized, structured, effi-cient. And while Sara had many of these traits as well, she lacked her mother's energy and drive. When it came to personality, she definitely took after her soft-spoken father.

Both of them loved her so much and only wanted what was best for her. *What is best for me, Lord? Why do I dread getting married like it was some sort of disease?*

She drove on, the late-morning sun bearing down on her and reminding her of past years when she didn't have a care in the world. Those memories used to encourage her. Now they only served as reminders of just how much she had failed.

TRAVIS THRASHER

Sara heard the cordless phone ringing but couldn't find it. It took her five rings to finally locate it underneath a small sofa cushion in her living room.

"Hello?" Sara asked in a tone that said, *You'd better not be selling anything.*

"Happy birthday, little lady."

"Hi, Bruce," she said, a smile coming over her lips.

"Has it been a good one so far?"

"Well, besides the fact that I'm thirty—yeah, I guess it has been."

"How's the new car?" Bruce asked her.

"Still as nice as it was when I drove you around."

"You want to drive tonight?"

"Sure. Where are we going?"

"It's a surprise. I just wanted to call and tell you I'm heading over—I'll be there in fifteen minutes. Is that okay?"

"Yeah, sounds great."

"See you soon."

Sara clicked off the phone and carried it to her bedroom. The alarm clock on her nightstand informed her that it was 6:45 P.M. Sara knew that meant Bruce would be knocking on her door at exactly 7:00.

Slightly flustered, she rummaged through a dresser drawer for a black slip. She usually ran a little late whenever she went out. Bruce, on the other hand, always arrived on time. Always. Sometimes it was scary how prompt he was. It was as though he sat outside the house waiting to hear his stopwatch go off.

But that's a silly thing to complain about—promptness, she told herself. *This birthday just has me in a bad mood. There's nothing wrong with being dependable. Nothing wrong with Bruce. He's a good guy.*

11 ≈ secrets

Bruce Erickson had first asked Sara out two years ago after a Sunday evening service at church. They had met in the singles' Sunday school class. But unlike many other women in that group, Sara wasn't looking for a boyfriend or a husband. She wanted Christian friends, male and female, and had decided that church would be a good place to find them. So when Bruce asked her out that first time, Sara told him no. She didn't lie to him or come up with some excuse. She simply told him that at the moment she wasn't ready to date. Bruce never asked her why but simply said okay and tried again two weeks later. Sara said yes that time, figuring it would be no big deal. An actual date with a decent guy might be nice for a change.

After several dates with him, Sara began to enjoy his company. It had been awhile since she had gone out with anyone, and Bruce was charming and likable. He was confident and extroverted, never letting the conversation drag or halt, but he was also genuinely interested in Sara. In fact, she could remember him mentioning the L-word on their fourth date. She hadn't said anything in response. It wasn't that she could never love him, but she just wasn't there yet. She wanted to take things slow.

Her mother, of course, had other assumptions. "I just adore him. Don't you?" she asked Sara one day when they met for lunch.

"He's a nice guy," Sara replied with a casual shrug.

"Well, he's certainly handsome, too. Not too tall, nice dark hair—looks perfect alongside you."

"Mom—"

"Honey, you've gone out several times now. Don't you think you should at least have him over for dinner?"

"I probably will. Just not yet."

Mom shook her head. "Why do you have this aversion to fine young men?"

That statement had hurt. Sara had looked at her mother's determined face and had almost begun to cry. Obviously her mother only wanted the best for her, but was Bruce necessarily the best?

"I'll call him, all right? I just don't have time this week."

"I just don't understand you sometimes, Sara." Her mother had walked to the ladies' room and left Sara sitting at the table, wishing she had never introduced her to Bruce.

That was the beginning of it all, the start of The Issue. The dating, marriage, family issue.

Sara could never explain it to her parents—that, as seemingly perfect as Bruce was, something wasn't there. Or more accurately, however perfect Bruce might be, he could never be someone else. That was the real problem.

And yet, for two whole years now she and Bruce had been dating, and they had even become what her mother called "an item." It was almost inevitable, when you thought about it. Dating for two years? Obviously, that was serious. With Sara and Bruce both being thirty? That was serious with a ton of implications to it. But Sara didn't like thinking about those implications—about things like the M-word, meaning marriage. Most of the time she managed to put the possibility completely out of her mind and just enjoy the simple dates and the nice friendship she had with Bruce.

Simple. Nice. Two words she thought about a lot in regard to Bruce. Maybe there's nothing wrong with settling for *simple* and *nice.*

The doorbell rang at exactly 6:59. Perfect timing as usual.

As Sara headed to the front door in her favorite black dress, she got the same feeling she always got before seeing Bruce. She couldn't describe it. It was neither good nor bad. It was . . . something.

The words resonated: *Simple. Nice. Simple. Nice.* Then she

chided herself. *Sara, you've got to snap out of this. Bruce is a great guy, and you know it. What's your problem, anyway?*

But she knew what her problem was.

She hesitated before opening the door. Yes, she knew why she hadn't fallen under the spell of Bruce the way so many others had. Others like her mother, who obviously couldn't wait for Sara to walk down the church aisle.

Her nose wrinkled in annoyance. What was the big hurry, anyway? she wondered. Why couldn't anyone be patient and understand?

Nobody understood because nobody knew.

Sara opened the front door to the familiar handsome face. "Hi," was all she managed to say.

Bruce looked at her and grinned. With a flourish he presented her with a single rose. "You look beautiful tonight. Happy birthday."

"Thanks."

Sara could hear her mother saying, "What a marvelous flower, Bruce." Sara found it ironic and even a bit sad that her mother was more impressed with Bruce than she was. Perhaps mothers were just that way. Bruce always said the right things to her mother. Then again, Bruce usually said the right things to everyone, including Sara. And she couldn't help but enjoy the compliments Bruce always gave her.

They went out to their favorite restaurant, an Italian place called Salvatore's. The restaurant was small and exclusive, and Bruce loved going there. Sara did love the food, but she always found the prices ridiculous. They had actually gone to Salvatore's for their first date. Sara had been a little overwhelmed.

"This is really expensive," Sara had said, looking at a simple bowl of pasta that cost more than thirty dollars.

But Bruce had told her she deserved a nice dinner like this. The fact of the matter was that Bruce owned a successful business employing about fifty people. He could afford thirty-five-dollar plates of pasta—and he told her exactly that. Modesty was not one of Bruce's strong points.

They sat at a small booth off to the side of the restaurant. Soft, romantic music floated around them as usual, yet something was different this night. Sara looked around. There didn't seem to be any other diners in the restaurant. She couldn't be certain at first, but after their meals arrived she could see that they were indeed alone, and she commented on it.

"That is odd, huh?" Bruce said, quickly changing the subject.

This was the first moment Sara suspected something was up, and she began to get a queasy feeling in the pit of her stomach. But Bruce said nothing, so she did her best to push her nervousness aside. What was she worried about anyway? Bruce was probably just planning one of his little expensive gestures—a birthday surprise. It couldn't be that bad. It would be nice, she told herself.

It happened after dessert. She ordered her favorite, of course—a slice of rich chocolate cheesecake. She ate it while Bruce drank his coffee. He almost never ate dessert.

"Sara, I've got a surprise for you," Bruce began, scaring Sara even more. "I arranged to have this restaurant all to ourselves."

"You what?" Sara asked with disbelief.

"This was the place we first came two years ago, when I barely knew your name yet was already in love with you. That's why I would like to do this here."

The waitress came out at that time. She presented Bruce with the bill and Sara with a gray suede box on a porcelain platter. Now Sara knew where this was headed, and all she could think about was escape. *Run,* Sara thought. *Run now, and don't look back.*

15 ≈ secrets

"Sara, would you please open that box?" he was saying as he put a hand on hers.

He really does love me, Sara told herself. *Do I deserve that love?*

She looked at Bruce and he smiled. His smile made her feel a little better. But her hands still shook as she opened the box to find an exquisite diamond solitaire in a platinum setting.

"Sara Anthony, I have been in love with you for the last couple of years. You know I have dreamt of spending the rest of my life with you. I can't wait any longer. Sara, will you marry me?"

Sara looked down at the sparkling stone and began crying uncontrollably. Of course, an elated Bruce came to her side and took her hand.

"It's okay, it's okay, you don't have to cry," he whispered to her. "I understand. I know you're happy."

But Sara continued to cry. Bruce *didn't* understand. How could he? She barely understood herself.

After a few minutes, she finally managed to control her sobs. Through tear-blurred eyes she saw Bruce kneeling on one knee beside her.

"I'm happy too," he said. "I love you, Sara."

She felt like she might faint any second. *I knew this was coming. But I still don't know what to do. What do I say now?*

"Well," he was asking her, "what do you say?" Strange how he could read her thoughts without having a clue as to what was in her heart.

As if you ever really gave him a chance, she reproached herself once more. Sara took a deep breath and looked at the ring again, then at his happy, eager face.

Bruce loved her, she knew he did. And they were a good match, she had to admit. They could have a good life. Maybe it was time to stop holding out for something that would never happen. All

TRAVIS THRASHER

those hopes and dreams—it was ridiculous to hang on to them for so many years. Something like this, someone like Bruce, might not come again. She had to face reality. And really, it probably wouldn't be so bad. Surely you could learn to love almost anybody . . . and Bruce was not so hard to love.

So with tears of regret that Bruce could not distinguish from those of joy, Sara nodded and spoke a word she didn't want to say but felt afraid not to: "Yes."

To Sara, the evening felt unbearably long, as if she were driving through a deep tunnel with her car lights turned off and the headlights from passing vehicles blinding her. After the proposal in Salvatore's, Bruce took Sara by his parents' house, then to her parents' house to make the grand announcements. Everyone gave them big hugs; the mothers cried, and Bruce's younger sisters all cried and jumped for joy. Sara's mom almost broke down in glorious shock. And Sara, caught up in the excitement, had almost convinced herself it was going to work.

When it was all over around midnight, Bruce gave Sara a tender farewell kiss at the door of her town home.

"I love you, Sara," he said. "We're going to be so happy."

Sara smiled up at him. "We *will* be happy," she replied firmly, and almost believed it herself.

But as she walked to her bedroom, Sara didn't believe her own words. Would they be happy? Would she? Could she be happy with Bruce? Could she ever learn to say the word, the L-word, to him and believe it in her heart?

That was when Sara broke down once again. She examined the ring on her shaking hand and started to cry. *Dear God,* she thought. *What have I done?*

Alone in her bedroom, she could hear the late-night sounds of crickets and cars even through the locked windows. *I shouldn't feel sad, Lord. There's no reason I should.*

The diamond glimmered in the dim light. Sara had always believed a ring like that would mean so much. Now, wearing it felt empty and even wrong.

Forgive me, Lord. I don't know what to think anymore.

For a few minutes she continued to weep, crying desperate tears only God above saw. When she regained her composure, Sara rose and went to her closet. She opened the door and began to rummage around. It took her awhile to find what she was looking for.

The shoe box was hidden in a larger box of school memorabilia and old childhood toys that was stuck in the corner of the closet. It had been literally years since she had opened it, but tonight she had to.

Inside the shoe box lay the contents of a life nobody knew about except Sara and one other. Contents of a love and a dream she had held in her heart for so many years. Now that love and those dreams could officially be considered over. She had waited so long for something that wasn't meant to be.

Letters, dozens of them, were bound with a crumbling rubber band. Several trinkets lay beside them—a necklace, a small leather band, a ridiculous pink heart. An envelope full of photos lay inside as well. Not many photos, but enough to stir the hope that had never really left her.

And, of course, the small, square case. She couldn't open it. Not yet. Not now. Not ever.

"I have trusted you, Lord," Sara prayed. "I have remained faithful to my word all these years. So why do I feel so horrible now? Why are you allowing these feelings to remain inside me? Why can't I move on and forget about him?"

TRAVIS THRASHER

She began sorting through the envelopes. Already, tears filled her eyes. How long had it been? How many years? How many lifetimes? How many nights had she dreamed for nothing? How many summer evenings had felt so bland because of remembered nights—remembered promises?

How many prayers had there been? So many—too many to count. "Give me peace, Lord," she whispered.

The letters were as she had left them long ago—in the order she had received them. There were so many.

On the night of her thirtieth birthday and her engagement, Sara Anthony felt miserable. Why did she always do this to herself? Why did she feel more lonely now than ever before?

Because you're angry, a voice inside her said. *You're angry at the one whom you've been praying to for years, praying daily for one thing. You're frustrated because those prayers have gone unanswered.*

But why? Why had those prayers seemingly gone unnoticed? Sara had searched her heart and her motives when praying. Perhaps she had fallen away from God's will in her life and didn't know it. She could remember the way she had been in grade school and high school—so sure of her faith, so on fire for the Lord. She had never felt lonely or empty then. Certainly there had been times when growing up hurt, but she had always been able to go to the Lord with her needs and her fears. She had always been able to pray to God for peace and for forgiveness.

How long had it been since her soul felt at rest? How long had it been since she prayed to God and felt his gentle calm cover her?

She knew it had everything to do with this box, with these memories. Perhaps the Lord was telling her to forget about them, to move on and get control over her life.

Maybe her prayers had been answered. Maybe God was telling her no.

But something made her believe that wasn't right. Somewhere, deep inside, she still believed. She still held on to a promise made years ago on a wintry day.

Remembering that promise, Sara took the first letter out of its envelope. Her shaking hands held the unfolded paper as she read. More tears fell.

She needed to do this. More than ever now that she was about to give up all hope for what she really wanted.

She began to read.

And remember.

Every sunrise blossoms with the memory of you.

dreams

MANY MILES from Atlanta, a young man meandered through the nighttime crowds at the pier and tried to make sense of his life. As he approached the festive gathering area cluttered with tables, an older woman accidentally knocked into him and slammed her entire cup of beer into his chest.

She cursed and apologized in the same breath. Ethan Ware looked at the heavyset woman and noticed the glazed look in her eyes. "That's okay," he said.

"Then watch where you're going," she snapped as she wandered off.

Lines of beer dripped down his shirt onto his shorts and legs. Ethan shook his head as he watched the lady waggle off into the crowd. He wrung out his shirt as best he could. The smell would turn sour in a few minutes, but few around him would notice or even care.

Just my luck. I go out for a nice walk and get doused by Ms. Friendly there, he thought with wry amusement.

He sat down at a table near the end of Navy Pier. A stone wall separated him from the dark and shifting waters of Lake Michigan. He faced the lit-up Chicago skyline, a sight that had never failed to excite him. Tonight, though, the familiar cityscape seemed strangely alien. As if everything had changed. Actually, when you thought about it, everything *had* changed. It was amazing how life could change so completely and still look so much the same.

What am I still doing here? he asked himself as he glanced down at the wet spot on his lap.

He had been outside walking ever since finishing his three-dollar dinner, a burrito and soda. It was close to nine now. Probably he should be back at his apartment doing something productive—something besides wandering.

But he still didn't have an answer. An answer to one of the most important decisions he would ever make.

He watched the crowd around him. A myriad of people sat at tables, drinking and talking and laughing. Families and couples walked along the pier. Others rode bikes or darted around on Rollerblades. Everyone looked so happy and content in the blinking, colorful lights of the pier.

Vaguely he wondered if he looked happy, too. What he felt was lonely.

"Can I get you anything?" a frantic waitress asked as she passed by.

How about a few answers? he thought. "Thanks. I'm okay," Ethan said.

He thought about the casual words he had uttered and was surprised by them. Was he indeed okay? And if so, why was he worrying so much about the decision that he had to make?

This is why I'm worrying so much. He took out the envelope from his back pocket and opened the letter. When had he received it? Five years ago? Perhaps. He took out the photo that rested inside and gazed at the dark-haired beauty who had sent him the letter. The smile in the photo still warmed him so many years later.

"Happy birthday, Sara."

If only he could talk to her and know how she was doing and tell

TRAVIS THRASHER

her how things were with him. If she still cared at all. But she was probably married, maybe even had children. As far as he knew, she could be living in downtown Chicago, walking the same streets he did every day. Or in China. Or in Timbuktu.

Do you ever think of me anymore? he wondered. *Has it been too long for you to still remember everything?*

Confusion seized him now, just like it had again and again during the past week. Why? Why now? Why after all this time? His big chance finally had come, and all he could think about was her.

Ethan wished he could ask his mother for advice. He would ask her every question his heart longed to know. Mom would know what to do. She always knew what to do. But now it was too late to ask Mom anything.

If only he had paid more attention to what she taught him as he was growing up. *I wish you were here, Mom.*

He thought about the last few years—more than a few, really—and about how much of a whirlwind his life had been in that span of time. Actually, it had been more like a tornado, wiping out almost everything in its path.

It had all started with his mother's death, he mused. Not before. He refused to call his father's abandoning their family the start of his downward spiral. He didn't want to give dear Dad that credit. And although their remaining family of two had had their share of problems when he was a teenager, they had also managed to hold each other together somehow. But then his mother's illness had finally taken its toll shortly after his graduation from college, and that was when the craziness had really begun.

He looked down at the photo, the most recent one he owned. It had been sent a few years after his mom died, before he and Sara finally lost touch. Sara's smile was dazzling, unchanging. He had memorized it long ago.

25 ≈ dreams

Ethan thought of his desperate proposal to Sara after his mother died, of the ache and emptiness he had felt when she said no. He had wandered around for a long time after that, trying to convince himself that this was what any writer with romantic sensibilities would do after having his heart broken. But hanging around bars and clubs until late hours of the night, sleeping the days away, living with college friends or friends of college friends, and not writing at all were neither romantic nor impressive. His actions were pathetic.

Finally, he had moved back to Chicago from the town where he'd gone to college and managed to get some stability in his otherwise superficial life. It had come in the form of a newspaper job and the friendship of two people.

Now, even those were gone.

Losing his job at the paper had been the first bit of bad news. He hadn't been exactly surprised, though, considering how competitive the journalism business was and how listlessly he'd approached the job. Besides, it barely paid anything, and there didn't seem to be much of a future in it. His dreams of writing a column for the paper had ended a long time ago, his lofty ideals about journalism and writing deteriorating when he realized his heart wasn't in it. He was still finding it hard to simply pick up a pen and jot down simple notes—and it was hard to be a writer for a paper when you could barely write anything. When the dismissal finally came a week earlier, Ethan had almost felt relieved.

Then his roommate and closest friend, Dennis, had decided to move out without any notice. Dennis was a likable and decent enough guy, but he had family difficulties and eventually they had taken their toll. Ethan could understand some of Dennis's problems, but he wished the timing had been a little different. Dennis had been one of the few people in Chicago Ethan spent time with. With Dennis gone, that left only one other tie to the city.

Unemployed and ready to find another place to live, Ethan had made the third big change himself—he had told Britanny he wanted to cool things off for a while. They had been going out for several months, but nothing much had developed in terms of a relationship. This breakup meant they would probably never talk to each other again. For him, it had been primarily a friendship, but Britanny wanted more.

He certainly understood that dilemma.

This all led up to the letter Ethan had received two days ago from one of the only relatives he stayed in touch with, his mother's brother. Uncle Pete in Germany somehow seemed to know how Ethan's life was going, so he had written to give him a proposition.

The letter from Germany was back in his apartment, not in his pocket, but he already knew its words by heart.

> *Ethan,*
> *Hope Chicago and the city life are treating you well! I wanted to let you know that our offer is still good, even after all this time. Considering the last few years, the change might be good for you. Think about it and let us know. We have a plane ticket with your name on it just waiting.*
> *We would love to see you. Our place is your place.*
> *Hope to hear from you soon. Call us anytime.*
>
> *Uncle Pete*

That letter had driven it home for Ethan. He needed to do something, anything, with his life. Chicago and the job and the apartment and Britanny had been okay, but he had grown up knowing life could be so much more than okay. Believing his own life

27 ≈ dreams

should be more. He needed to move on, and Uncle Pete's offer could be just the chance he needed.

Yet Ethan could still only think of one thing: *Find her.*

This was foolish, of course. It had been years, many years, since he last saw Sara—almost as many years ago as his mother's death. She had her life now, one in which he no longer belonged, one he could hardly imagine. And what if he did find her? What would he say or do? What else could he say that hadn't been said? He had told her everything in the last letter, and her silence had been a clear response. Enough had been said. Obviously her decision had been made.

Now he thought about the decision he had to make. The offer from his uncle and aunt in Germany to come live with them and work in his uncle's business seemed incredibly tempting. He couldn't stop thinking about the offer, about taking advantage of that one-way plane ticket to Germany his uncle had offered and getting away for a long time—at least two or three years. But what did he have to lose, anyway? He had no real ties to anyone here. In fact, he really had very little, especially in the form of inspiration. Perhaps the one-way plane ticket would be good for him. Good for him and his dreams.

He had always dreamed of traveling to Europe.

As he looked around at the never-ending busyness of the pier, Ethan thought back to his younger days—back when his mom had still been alive, when Sara had been a part of his life, when he had known exactly what he wanted—or at least thought he knew. Everyone he ever met heard about his dreams: dreams of traveling around the world, of writing books, of finding the right person to share it all with. He had been convinced that he would achieve all those dreams and more. Now, so many years later, the only thing he could say for certain was that he had found the right person for him. But maybe he wasn't the right one for her. As for the rest of those dreams, they appeared long gone and certainly impossible.

Impossible? he thought in horror. *How can I even dare to think that?*

He looked again at the photo of Sara and realized he needed to see her at least one more time. He needed to know why she had remained silent for so long.

And if she still remembered the promise she had given him so many years ago.

*All I have to do to see you
again is close my eyes. . . .*

plans

"IS EVERYTHING OKAY?"

Sara coughed on her steak and waved a hand that said everything was. Bruce looked worried for a second, until she took a breath and managed a reassuring smile.

"Sorry. Wrong pipe."

And she said nothing more. She had said very little for most of the evening, ever since Bruce came to pick her up for another round of "Let's Plan This Marriage!"

She had tried. She really had. But the plans, the preparations, the endless conversations, the ideas and suggestions, and the decisions all worried her. Especially the decisions. Why did a wedding have to involve so many?

Ethan used to tell her she worried too much, that she spent too much time making decisions. And he had been right. She hated this about herself. "Sometimes you have to just let it all go," Ethan had told her once. "Life's too short to be worrying all the time."

Staring at the imploring face of her fiancé, Sara found herself wishing for a bit of Ethan's carefree attitude. She wondered if he still viewed life the same way. "Every day is a new opportunity to do something really crazy and get away with it." That had been Ethan's motto, one he would always state with his fiery and adorable grin.

33 ≈ plans

She had loved that about him. She had loved virtually everything about him.

Well, now I'm about to do something really crazy. I'm about to say goodbye to one of the nicest guys I've ever known. If I could only figure out how to say it. . . .

Now, one week after saying yes to Bruce's proposal, Sara sat at dinner remembering Ethan and trying to figure out a way to tell Bruce no. She had to stop this nonsense before it became worse.

Everybody seemed to have lost their minds. Bruce never stopped talking about Their Future and Their House and Their Picket Fence with Their Dog Toto. It seemed that he couldn't even greet Sara without saying, "And after we get married. . . ." Her father seemed content and passive, as usual, but he would talk to Bruce about the wedding, too. And her mother already seemed headed for a mental hospital at the rate she was going, dealing with all the Wedding Plans.

There were all sorts of things to think about: the date and time of the wedding, where she would buy her dress, what the cake would look like, who the attendants would be, who would be invited (and of course, Aunt Lizzie would have to come, Mom said), where they would go on their honeymoon, what colors the flowers and dresses and shoes would be, whether guests would throw rice or birdseed or flower petals, and on and on.

Things that crowded her mind every time she closed her eyes.

Things that held no real interest to Sara.

In spite of all the excitement, Sara had found it hard to muster up any sort of enthusiasm. And worse than that, she had even more doubts now than she had a week ago. She had assumed that as time went by and the realization of her decision sank in, she would get used to the idea of marrying Bruce. But that wasn't happening.

TRAVIS THRASHER

She had to tell him the truth. She *would* tell him the truth. Right here, over dinner.

"You're quiet tonight. Everything okay?"

Sara smiled and was about to say something, but Bruce spoke again. "Because if you don't like December 26, we can change, you know. I know it's an odd date."

An odd date summed it up, all right. But her parents had married on that date and had always said they wanted Sara to do the same. She simply had to have a Christmas wedding. So Sara, compliant as usual, had agreed and said little.

"The date is fine," Sara said.

The date wasn't the problem. The wedding itself was the problem.

She wished she had the school and her little kindergartners to cheer her up. But with summer here, there was nothing to divert her attention from the wedding. She hadn't even told anyone at first—her friends or her fellow teachers at school—about her engagement. Only after her mother insisted had she called people and made the announcement.

Not exactly the typical, enthusiastic bride-to-be.

"Bruce, I've been thinking . . . ," she began.

"About what?"

"About this, everything. I don't know. I'm . . . uh, sort of nervous."

"I'm nervous, too. But we've still got awhile to let things sink in."

"Aren't we . . . aren't we moving a bit fast?"

Bruce fidgeted in his chair and looked at her. "How so?"

"I just think all these decisions and everything—can't we wait on some of them?"

"Like the date?"

35 ≈ plans

Try the whole thing, Sara thought. But she still couldn't bring herself to come right out and say it. "Like lots of things."

"Sara, what's wrong?"

Could she change her mind now? Of course she could. Of course she could give the ring back and explain to Bruce about her reservations. And of course Bruce would be loving and sensitive, and then take himself and his expensive ring and his thoroughly decimated ego and leave her forever. And her mom—well, her mom would perhaps take the convertible out and wave good-bye to Sara and drive off the nearest cliff.

Better now than later, surely. It had only been one week. It couldn't be that bad saying no. Why had she said yes in the first place? But of course she'd had to say yes. What else could she say? How could she turn down a man who was, in her mother's words, "a perfect guy"?

Sara thought of Bruce and the reasons she enjoyed spending so much time around him. He was great with kids. He spent many evenings helping her grade papers. He always complimented her and encouraged her and rarely, if ever, got angry. He was stable and responsible and always seemed to be thinking of the future.

There really was nothing wrong with Bruce. Maybe something was wrong with her. . . .

But what about love? a voice inside her asked. *What about love?* This was the same voice that had been haunting her all week. A voice that whispered one thing over and over: *Do you love him?*

And the answer, of course, was yes. Certainly she loved him. He was a brother in Christ. He was a good friend, a pleasant companion. He was good to her, and she cared about him. But Sara knew this wasn't the love that the voice was asking about, wasn't the love that Bruce wanted or expected or deserved. That kind of love was the kind she had experienced only once in her life.

TRAVIS THRASHER

She had wondered recently whether feelings that strong could ever come back to her again.

"Sara, please," Bruce said, his face distressed. "Talk to me."

Tell him now, the voice inside urged. But when she looked into his kind brown eyes, the corners furrowed in concern, somehow she just couldn't.

"I-I'm just not feeling good right now. It's just . . . just a bit too much. . . ."

"Is it me? Did I do anything?"

"Oh, no," she replied. "It has nothing to do with you." And that, of course, was part of the problem.

She excused herself and walked to the ladies' room.

Please, Lord, help me to know what to say, to know what to do. Should I marry Bruce? Is it wrong for me to marry him when I really want someone else? Or am I just hanging on to something that wasn't right in the first place?

Did God have one single person picked out for her from the beginning of time? She used to believe this and had held on to this belief for so many years. And she had always assumed Ethan Ware was the one. She had believed that somehow there would be a miracle, that they would be together. But that belief was starting to fade away.

Where could Ethan be? After all these years, she still desperately missed him. And she had kept her word—she had continued to pray for him, every day in fact, yet she didn't have a clue whether it made any difference.

Maybe she would never find out.

She leaned against the cool, tile wall as pangs of hurt and guilt swept over her again. She believed she had made the right decision years ago, but that didn't lessen the painful memories. She had been the one to say no, to force the goodbye. It had been her decision, all hers.

So why, then, did she find it so difficult to move on?

She had made Ethan a promise, and she had kept it. But she had no reason to believe he had kept his promise to her. And no reason to believe she should let those long-ago promises determine the course of her life.

So where did that leave her? Thirty years old and trying to face the fact that she was about to enter a marriage with quite a lot of doubts and with very little passion.

But maybe that's what marriage should be about, Sara told herself. Stability. Comfort and companionship. And children—Sara certainly wanted children, and Bruce would be a wonderful father.

Maybe her mother was right. This might be one of the only opportunities a great guy like Bruce would come around. She could learn to live with him and maybe even learn to love him. He might not ever be like Ethan, but who could as far as she was concerned?

Her dear, sweet Ethan. Would anyone ever compare to him or to the memory of him?

Why, oh dear God, why did he forget?

I still dream of being with you.

insights

ETHAN KNOCKED on the apartment door belonging to his landlord, a crusty and talkative old man named Herb. The door opened to reveal Herb in ankle-high black socks, white shorts, and a worn Chicago Bears T-shirt that said "Super Bowl Champs." The man smiled at Ethan and told him to come in.

"This is the rent money for the rest of the summer," Ethan said, handing Herb an envelope.

"Don't have to pay it all at once, you know." Herb's deep voice sounded scratchy as usual.

"Our lease goes through August. I wanted to make sure you got the money—Dennis gave me his remaining share. He moved out a couple of weeks ago."

"Yeah, he said something about that. You moving too?"

Ethan shook his head. "I don't know, to be honest. I've got an opportunity somewhere."

"Somewhere? Where's somewhere? Here, sit down, come on. Want anything to drink?"

"No, thanks." Ethan sat on the edge of a musty sofa. He was used to half-hour conversations with Herb.

"So where's this somewhere?"

"Europe. I've got an uncle in Germany who's been trying for a while to get me to work for him."

"I've never been to Europe. Always wanted to go, you know. So, when do you leave?"

Ethan shrugged. How could he tell Herb, of all people, his dilemma? That's how things worked for him. Most people had relatives, best friends, or even a psychiatrist to give them advice. When Ethan needed advice, he seemed to get it from people like Herb.

"I'm debating about taking a trip before I go."

"A trip, huh? Myself, I haven't been out of Chicago for fifteen years. I keep on saying I'll go, but then I never get the chance, not with this building and all that. Why do you wanna take a trip before you leave? Ain't Germany good enough?"

Ethan looked at Herb, lounging in a Lazyboy chair and sipping a cup of coffee. "To see an old friend."

"Ah, a girl, I bet," Herb said, revealing yellow teeth. "You know, I was married once. Long time ago."

Ethan nodded, trying to show an interest.

"Yeah, a long time ago. She passed on. She was my high school sweetheart, you know. They're the best. Doreen. That was her name. Died of cancer."

"I'm sorry," Ethan replied.

Herb waved a hand. "So, what's your girl's name?"

"Well, I don't really—"

"Come on," Herb urged.

"Her name is Sara. But I don't know—I haven't seen her in years. She's probably married and all that. I really don't know."

"What don't you know?"

"It's been too long," Ethan said. "Too many years since I saw her. And the last time I wrote to her, I never heard back."

Herb laughed. "What a sorry sap. You don't know whether to go see her?"

"I don't even know *where* to go."

Herb continued to chuckle. Ethan stared at him, irritated. Here he was telling this goofy man his troubles, and all he was getting were guffaws. That and a strange odor coming from the kitchen.

"Look, Son. Do you love this girl? That's the only question you need to know."

"Well, yeah. Of course. I've always loved her."

"Did you tell her that? Most guys have a hard time with that word."

"Not me. She knows."

"Then what's your problem? Go find her."

"It's not as simple as that."

"No?" Herb asked, stretching over to rub his foot. "Let me tell you the story Doreen used to like telling others. She was religious, my Dorie, and she liked to preach to me all the time. She was a sweetie, but her preaching got a little old. Anyways, I had to wait for years before she'd finally agree to marry a fella like me. We were different, her and me. But everyone's different, right?"

Ethan nodded and thought, *What am I doing here?*

Herb continued. "Dorie always told me that if Jacob from the Bible could wait for seven years just to marry his wife, then I could certainly wait a year or two. Patience, Dorie told me. Of course, I was thinking I just might die if I had to wait seven years, but Dorie finally gave in. She finally said yes."

I wish it was as easy as that, Ethan thought.

"So you gotta be patient. You gotta be like that Jacob fella that worked and waited all those years. How long's it been for you?"

Ethan wasn't even sure. Eight, perhaps nine years? No, it was right after his mother died. . . .

"Eight years, I think," he said.

The man rubbed his foot again and nodded. "Hey, that's okay. You still gotta be patient. What—you wanna marry this girl?"

"Yeah, I do," Ethan said without hesitating.

"Then go, boy. Find her. You're only young once. Find her and ask her. You gotta know."

"There's one problem."

"What's that?" Herb asked.

"I already found her once and asked her to marry me. But she said no."

"Oh. Well, I guess that could be a problem. What, she doesn't love you?"

Ethan smiled. "She did love me. That's what she said. But things were—they were complicated."

Herb finished his cup of coffee and lowered the footrest of his Lazyboy. He pushed himself to his feet, scratching the back of his neck. "Sure you don't want anything to drink? Soda? Coors?"

"No." Ethan stood up to leave. "I really should go."

"Where're you going to go?" Herb asked him.

"Like I said, things are complicated."

Herb walked Ethan to the door. The man looked up at Ethan and gave him another yellow-toothed smile. "Y'know, there's not a day goes by that I don't wish I was thirty or forty years younger. I dream about it, sitting around here collecting rent checks. That's why I do this—you know that? So I can see you young people all the time. It keeps me going."

Ethan nodded and stepped out the door.

Herb stood in the doorway, a clump of his sparse hair sticking out from one side of his head. "Look, Son. I never deserved Dorie. I guess us guys never really deserve the women we love. But it's worth it. The waiting, I mean. And the trying. Like that Jacob fella."

Ethan shook Herb's hand. "Take care," he said.

TRAVIS THRASHER

"Listen to your heart, Son," Herb called when Ethan was halfway down the hallway.

Back in the apartment, Ethan stared at the suitcases near the door. He was ready to go—but where? Was he going to try to find Sara? To risk another round of rejection?

Things are different now, he thought. But apparently that hadn't made any difference. Did she just stop caring? *She knows everything, yet she never said a word. Not a single word.*

Most likely she didn't know what to say. She'd gone on with her life, and he didn't fit in it.

He could see himself knocking on a door to a happy household. Sara would answer and greet him in a polite manner and show him wedding pictures and baby pictures and pictures of her happy, fulfilled life. What would he do then? Make up something about how he just happened to be in the neighborhood, "Just passing by the state of South Dakota, don't you know"? Tell her he was happy for her?

He could be happy for her, he thought. He loved her that much—loved her enough to be glad that she was happy. Or at least he thought he did.

But how could he live without knowing for sure?

He noticed his answering machine still plugged into the wall and saw the blinking message button. His breath stopped as he pressed it. *Please let it be her,* he silently prayed, even as he told himself it couldn't possibly be. *Let it be her, please let it be her.*

"Hey, Ethan, this is Andy again," the electrified voice on the machine told him. "I'm downtown for a couple of days. Man, you're hard to find, you know that? Anyway, give me a call as soon as you can. It'd be great to hang out."

45 ≈ insights

Ethan found a pen and the back of a used envelope and wrote down the number Andy had given.

Not a good sign, Ethan thought. *I pray and it ends up being Andy. Is that some kind of bad joke?* Andy's voice brought back a wave of memories. How many months had it been since he last heard it? Could it have been more than a year ago?

I haven't told Andy about everything that's happened. I thought he was gone for good. Memories of the dark days of college and the darker ones in the following years seemed to belong to another person, yet they also seemed to have only happened yesterday. Recollections of that long period in his life still stung. They hung above him like murky clouds on a sunny day.

"Andy," Ethan said out loud as if to verify he had just heard the message.

Andy had been one of his closest friends during college, during the time in his life when his mother's health had wavered and there had only been a handful of people he could even relate to. On one end of the spectrum had been his beloved Sara, who encouraged him through her letters, who kept a light shining for him. And on the other end had been Andy, who had helped him take his mind off the painful realities of his life.

Perfect timing, Ethan thought. *A couple of nights out with Andy would make me forget about everything else.* He looked around and thought for a moment. He picked up the phone to call.

Don't do it, another voice said. *That's the last thing you need.*

He dialed the numbers anyway and waited. A voice answered at the other end.

Ethan knew exactly what he would say.

*. . . with a smile that could
melt the coldest of hearts.*

words

SARA FOLDED the pages of the letter and slipped them back into the worn envelope. She wiped her eyes and wondered if she should keep reading. *This is so foolish,* she told herself. *Why can't I just grow up?*

Letters lay scattered around her on the bed. Though years had passed, Ethan's letters never failed to move her. His words always filled her with a sense of vulnerability, the kind she might blush over. She had never considered herself to be particularly interesting, so when the letters came asking her to describe her life and her feelings, she had been unsure what to say. She'd felt plain, sensible, and ordinary. What could she say that would be of any interest to a spontaneous and carefree person like Ethan?

Everything, he would implore. He had wanted to know anything and everything.

So she had told him about babysitting jobs and her child-development classes and her friends and her church activities. And to her amazement, Ethan had been impressed with her letters. He had always declared his awe at her life, even though his own was one wild and crazy adventure after another. His own letters told her of his excursions to different places, either with friends or by himself. They enthused about his many different interests—soccer, nature, track, drums, art, skiing—while they also detailed his lack of enthusiasm for anything pertaining to growing up or schoolwork or responsibilities.

"I never want to grow up, Sara," he had once written to her. "When I grow up, I want to live like I'm having a midlife crisis."

He had described to her the details of getting in trouble for doing simple and stupid things—like swimming in a neighbor's pool at midnight and driving over the college's soccer field with his car. Episodes like these still made her laugh and shake her head. Ethan would write things like "I guess that really wasn't a good idea" and then draw a smiley face to show his amusement. Her own letters paled in comparison to his. She always felt she had nothing to tell him except for dull details of her ho-hum life. But Ethan had claimed to find her "constant" attitude regarding life remarkable.

"That's what I like about you," he had written once. "You are responsible, and you think through the things you do. I need somebody like that."

And of course, he had never failed to remind her how much he admired her enduring faith. . . .

A lot of good that did us, she thought crossly as she tucked the letter away.

It was her lunch with Elyse that had sent Sara back to the old letters once again. Or rather, it was something Elyse had said during lunch.

Elyse Barry was one of Sara's closest friends—a fellow school-teacher she had met in the church singles group. The outgoing and attractive blonde had been the one to invite Sara to the women's small group she loved attending on Wednesdays.

Elyse was also one of the only people she had told about Ethan.

So that afternoon, between bites of Caesar salad and crusty French bread, Sara had shared some of her mixed feelings with

Elyse. It felt good to tell somebody about what she was going through, to have someone listen and understand.

But Elyse had also said something that stuck with Sara the rest of the day. "There's nothing wrong with remembering someone you once loved," she had said. "You just have to figure out if you still love Ethan—and if you can ever have feelings like that for Bruce."

That comment had sent Sara back once more to Ethan's old letters. She had told herself she wouldn't do this again. But Elyse was right. There was nothing wrong in remembering the past.

But it's wrong to be stuck in the past. And wrong to keep all of this from Bruce.

Strange feelings still plagued her, and she needed to make sense of them. It was odd that, the more time that went by since her engagement, the more she thought of Ethan. Before, she had been able to banish him fairly easily from her everyday thoughts. Now, she was always seeing his mischievous smile, his brilliant blue eyes, his wavy hair falling against his forehead. She could hear his voice as she read his words, some written more than ten years earlier.

Stop this now, Sara told herself.

She opened another letter. Just one more. Just one.

The distinguishing characteristic of Ethan's letters had been the name he put on the front corner of the envelope where return addresses were usually written. He'd called himself everything from James Dean to Han Solo to Your Secret Pen Pal.

The envelope she held now, though, simply said Ethan. *I remember this one,* Sara thought.

She unfolded the page.

> *My dearest Sara,*
>   *Weeks ago I wondered if I could feel any worse about life. Yesterday I discovered I could.*

51 ≈ words

I can't say I agree with you, but I understand. And I want you to know that my promise will never die, that I will always love you. These aren't vain words, either. I mean them, Sara. I mean them with my whole heart.

I never thought things would end up like this. I really thought we could work it all out. I still don't know what to think about all the things you said—I simply find it impossible to believe all of that. But I will say this. Meeting you in Hartside years ago— that wasn't just chance. I don't know who or what put us together, but I know our paths were meant to cross.

And I believe they're meant to cross again. I won't give up hope.

I won't give up loving you, either.

Ethan

Sara cried and remembered receiving that letter years ago. It had been the final one he had sent to her, the final word from Ethan.

Their paths hadn't crossed again.

What had happened? Where had he gone?

She had sent him a letter back, asking him to read the Bible she had once given him. She had heard nothing since then. Perhaps he had finally decided enough was enough.

Sara bundled the letters together once more, tucked them away in the nightstand, and wandered downstairs. On the coffee table was a stack of wedding invitations to be addressed, on the floor a stack of bridal magazines her mom had brought over. The miniature clock on an end table told her it was close to five o'clock. She would be meeting Bruce at her parents' house for dinner at six.

Her parents still knew nothing about her ambivalence. Neither did Bruce, though surely he wondered about her lack of enthusiasm. And everything was escalating—plans, schedules, details.

Everything was building, and all Sara could do was dream about Ethan.

These feelings needed to go somewhere. But where?

Sara ended up in her kitchen by the sink, gazing through the lace-trimmed window at the lush green plants on her patio, enjoying the silence. She had been over at her parents' house so much recently; it felt good to be back in her own place. Standing there in the quiet, Sara lifted her thoughts toward God, asking for direction. And then she prayed for Ethan, just as she had done almost daily for the last eight years. She prayed that he would find the truth, that he would find his way to the Lord. He had been on the verge so many times—Sara knew he had been. He had told her. He was so close, and everything in his life seemed to be leading him that way.

But would he ever find his way? Or were all the prayers for nothing?

Sara had never understood how somebody who could believe in her and in a love that seemed so impossible could not believe in a God who had brought the two of them together. Ethan had been blunt about his lack of belief when they first met so many years ago. In some of his letters he had asked questions about what she believed—he had seemed genuinely interested. In others, he had denied everything—God's existence, his love, his control, his Son. There could not be a God, he had blustered—not in a world like this. Sometimes Ethan had seemed defiant in his unbelief, especially after his mother died. Over the years, he had grown more ardent in his feelings for Sara and more passionate about his disregard for his God. And that was why she had told him no.

That was why she could not marry him, why the love Ethan believed in so passionately could not move forward. Oh, she loved

53 ≈ words

him, too; Ethan would never understand just how deeply she loved him. She had told him that.

No, love had never been the problem in their relationship. The problem was one of doing what was right, doing what the Bible taught her, doing what the Lord required of his people.

Of course, she couldn't forget the promise made to a dying woman. "Promises," Sara uttered in frustration. She had made promises years ago, always thinking everything would work out in the end.

She had dared to hope that things would change and that then their life together would be the kind she had dreamed about. He would tell her he had finally said yes to the God who loved him more than she did. Then she would tell him how she had prayed every night for his soul, for his safety, for his life. And they would both marvel at God's goodness and live happily ever after.

In the silence, Sara reflected on God's goodness. She knew she had doubts, plenty of doubts. And she knew that she wasn't a perfect Christian, either. Not while she was carrying these secrets around, deceiving her parents and Bruce and a lot of other people. Then there was the worry. And the guilt. And the love she still carried deep in her heart.

Was she wrong to wonder where Ethan might be?

She waited, but she heard no answers. She knew some questions never get answered.

If only she could see him one more time. If only she could have one more chance to listen to his voice, to hear him say something, anything.

And then as she stood in her kitchen peering out the window, an idea came. In one second it all came to her. It made perfect sense.

The decision was made. Sara knew what she had to do.

PART 2

*You loved me enough to
never give up on me.*

encounters

IN THE SUMMER between her sophomore and junior years of high school, Sara Anthony had vowed never to date another boy again.

She knew she had high expectations. Yet that hadn't stopped her from going out with several guys from her high school during her first two years there. They were older than she was, they played football and basketball, they always had dozens of girls swooning all over them. She had given them a chance, and each one had let her down.

Yet even more disappointing than that, Sara felt she had let herself down. Her expectations didn't have anything to do with the kind of car her date drove or how high he rated on the popularity scale or how many sports he played. She wanted someone who made her laugh like her father did, someone who really listened when she talked about anything and everything, someone who felt as passionate about the Lord as she did.

She wondered if there were any guys out there like that. After her short and painful attempts at dating, Sara decided she wasn't going to meet any. It seemed simpler to give up on that scene altogether.

On the first day of Hope Springs summer camp outside Hartside, North Carolina, her resolve had been tested, but only briefly, when a good-looking, tanned senior from Georgia asked if she wanted to take a walk after the evening service.

"Where to?" Sara asked in a polite but direct tone.

"Uh, you know, around," the senior replied, obviously surprised by her response.

"No, thanks," she told him. "I've probably already been there."

Her response left the openmouthed senior speechless—and Sara feeling a bit guilty. She hadn't meant to be rude or arrogant, but she didn't want to think about guys—especially not at this camp. She'd broken up with one boyfriend just a month earlier because he had lied to her about dating other girls, and he had justified it by saying he was just a guy. And that was the kind of person Sara seemed to attract: "Sorry, I didn't mean to lie to you, but I'm just a guy." These were the sort of guys she fell for, and they had humiliated her more than once.

No more, she told herself.

This was her first time at the Christian camp, located several hours from her home in Tennessee. Hope Springs camp meant a lot of things to a lot of people, but for Sara, it was a place to get to know other Christians from both her church and the surrounding churches in the South. For one week, campers would enjoy the beauty of the Great Smoky Mountains as they spent the days and evenings in outdoor activities, fun social events, and Bible study and worship. It would be a wonderful break from the otherwise boring summer and would put a lot of good distance between her and Mr. "I'm Just a Guy."

The camp's location was exactly what she'd hoped for—a collection of small log cabins all nestled in the arms of a great wooded mountain. The nearby town of Hartside, located just minutes from the Tennessee border, lay at the foot of the mountain, about ten minutes from their cabins. Hartside was a quaint tourist town with a hotel, several bed-and-breakfasts, a miniature main street with shops and restaurants, and a cluster of homes—perfect for afternoon excursions. Apart from the town, the area consisted of woods and mountains and small vacation cabins similar to the ones the campers were staying in.

Perfect for getting away.

There were probably more than sixty teenagers attending the camp. At least ten were assigned to each cabin, depending on its size. Guys from Tennessee churches might be in one house, girls from Western North Carolina churches in another, and so on. They alternated meetings between a small church several miles down the road and a campground in the other direction.

After the first evening service, which consisted of singing hymns and reading the Bible and listening to one of the pastors speak, Sara decided to take the tanned, good-looking guy's advice and go for a walk. She did it alone, however, setting out along one of the dirt roads that the camp leader had pointed out as "within bounds" for campers.

As the sun slipped down toward the mountains in the west, Sara walked along the road and became lost in her thoughts. Once again she began thinking of her life and whether or not she would ever meet Mr. Right. She told herself such a person didn't exist, but at the same time she longed for someone who would genuinely love her and care for her. She wanted someone who was passionate about life and the Lord, someone who would inspire her to forget all of life's worries and letdowns.

Will I ever meet a guy like this, Lord? Am I wrong to want someone like this?

God would show her one day. Deep in her heart, she believed it and trusted him. She enjoyed walks like this, where she thought and prayed and conversed with God. A voice never came back, booming down a "YES, DO THAT, SARA" or even whispering in the winds. But Sara almost always felt a peace inside her when she prayed to the Lord. She felt a similar peace now. A sense that everything would truly be all right.

After ten minutes of walking, Sara found herself looking up at an unfamiliar log cabin perched on a hill above her. A steep, winding driveway curled up to the sweet, two-story home with a deck that overlooked the mountains to the west.

Sara stopped and gazed up at the house. *Is this one of the cabins the camp is renting out?* Sara wondered.

For a few minutes, Sara stared up at the cabin and saw nothing. There was no sign of life. One of the camp managers had said that some of the houses around Hartside were owned by Floridians who visited on and off during the year. Perhaps this cabin was one of those.

She stood there for several long minutes, considering, then ventured partway up the winding drive. She didn't see a single car, and the flower boxes on the deck were obviously untended. Pine needles and decaying leaves cluttered the drive. Surely nobody had been home for a while.

Maybe it was being away from home, or the beautiful clear evening sky, or the recent prayer she had lifted up to the heavens. Whatever it was, Sara felt compelled to walk the rest of the way up to the cabin and stand on the deck.

She told herself the view would be worth risking embarrassment if an owner were to find her there.

What a view it was.

The surrounding mountains rolled off into the distance in every direction. The tops of their thick trees looked comfortable enough to lie down on. Distant clouds seemed to hover above the peaks, with shadowy outlines of mountains farther behind them. God wasn't merely evident in this panoramic display before her; he seemed to be living and breathing all around her.

Sara stared at the view in front of her and said another prayer out loud. "Dear Father, thank you for the incredible beauty of your creation. Thank you for all you give to us. And all you've given to me. Thank you for always being there, and for—"

"Hey."

Sara felt her heart roll up into her mouth as she let out a gasp. She turned around and saw a boy about her age standing behind her on the deck, smiling.

"Who are you talking to?" he asked her.

Sara took a deep breath and composed herself. "I was—what are you doing? Did you follow me?"

She was trying to remember if she had seen this boy earlier that day. He didn't look familiar.

"Follow you?" he asked.

"Yes, from camp."

"Yeah, that's exactly what I did. I've been following you. I always follow girls out in the wilderness to spy on them."

From his tone, Sara knew he was kidding. But who was he? She thought she would have remembered him from camp, even if she wasn't making it a point to check out the guys. His wide, slightly crooked smile almost made her laugh, for no reason at all. His blue eyes looked fun loving and luminous, saying as much as his words had. He looked friendly. Whoever he was, she felt comfortable—if a little bit breathless.

"Nice view, huh?" he asked her.

"Yes, it is."

"Who were you talking to?" he asked again.

"Who was I—oh, I was praying."

He nodded and raised his eyebrows but remained quiet.

63 ≈ encounters

"I don't think I saw you at camp today. Where are you from?"

"Chicago," he said.

"Chicago? Seriously?"

"No, I'm lying. Not only do I spy on girls in the evening, but I also make a point of lying to them."

Sara laughed. "No, it's just—that's a long way to come for camp."

"Camp?"

"You're here for camp, right?"

The boy laughed. He walked to the edge of the deck and sat on the railing, more than three stories above the drop-off below. "I live here."

Sara felt sick. *This has to be a joke, right? Of course it is. He's joking around.* But his eyes met hers, and she couldn't tell whether he was joking or not.

"You're not from the camp?"

He shook his head. "Nope. Never attended a camp in my life. Well, I think maybe Cub Scouts or something like that, but I got booted out. Can you believe that? Getting kicked out of Cub Scouts. I was scarred for life."

Sara laughed again. "You really live here? In this cabin?"

"Well, for the time being. I really do live in Chicago. My mom and I are—we're taking a vacation of sorts." He locked his legs around the wood railing and leaned out over it. "Ahhhhhhhhh."

"Don't do that. Are you crazy?"

"This wood is hard as a rock. It's not going anywhere."

"I'm sorry I'm—" Sara stopped, unsure what to say. "I'm sorry I just walked up here."

"I don't care. Not like we get many visitors."

Sara still felt embarrassed, but curiosity filled her. "What do you do up here?"

"I'm beginning to learn how to talk to groundhogs. They have a primitive language, but I think I'm finally starting to break through."

Again, Sara laughed. She couldn't recall the last time she had met someone so sarcastic and funny. Who was this guy?

"Actually," he said, "I don't do much of anything except read and write."

"You like writing?"

He hesitated before answering, a reaction that seemed to contradict his outgoing personality. "Yeah," he said, "I do."

Sara looked up and saw his face outlined by the colors of the fading sun behind him. "I should go. It's getting late."

"You don't have to go. Like I said, my conversations with the groundhogs haven't been as fulfilling as I had hoped they would be."

"No, I really have to. We have a curfew. At the camp, I mean."

At first, he didn't say anything as she began to walk away. Then she heard his voice call out to her. "Wait a minute."

"What?" she asked.

"What's your name?"

Sara blushed, thankful the light was fading.

"Sara. Sara Anthony."

"Well, Miss Anthony. I'm Ethan Ware. Feel free to visit our deck anytime. For the view, or to pray, or to do whatever."

She nodded and thanked him. She thought about mentioning the evening services at camp to him, but she felt stupid and decided to not say anything.

That night, on the first night of her Hope Springs camp experience, after vowing not to have anything to do with guys whatsoever, Sara dreamed of Ethan Ware.

I felt totally alone, and I finally realized that nothing or no one could fill that emptiness.

prayers

ETHAN SLICED his finger on the open can of soup and let loose with a loud curse he had been storing for a while.

His mother, sitting only a foot away at the table, looked at him with disappointment. "Ethan, please. Don't swear."

"Blame the soup can. Besides, I'm getting sick of soup for lunch every day. Can't we go out occasionally? Get a hamburger or something?"

"You know we're on a budget."

He looked at her with frustration in his eyes and shook his head. "So, are we going to be on a budget for the rest of our lives?"

"Ethan, you know how things are."

"Not really, Mom. How are things, really? You never want to talk about what's going on."

"I don't know what to tell you."

"What to tell me? Okay, then, how about this? What's up with Dad? I mean, really. What's going on?"

Marietta Ware looked down at the table and said nothing.

"I hate him," Ethan said.

"Ethan, stop that now. Please stop."

"Well, I do. I can't help it. He never did love us—"

Ethan stopped when he saw his mother break down again, this time with heaving sobs that even he couldn't ignore. He rushed to his mother's side, kneeling before her and holding on to her knees.

"I'm sorry, Mom. I'm sorry. I shouldn't have said anything. I'm just so mad at him. But I didn't mean to hurt you. Mom, please . . ."

"It's okay, honey," Marietta said as she tried to compose herself.

"I can't believe he just left us like that. I still can't. I-I hate him for doing this to us, especially to you."

"Sweetheart, he's just lost."

"No, don't do that," Ethan said, pulling back.

"Honey, it's true."

He shook his head. "Don't give me any of that Christian junk. Not now. I don't want to hear it."

"We can still pray for him, Ethan."

"I'm not praying anymore. I've prayed enough. What does that get us? Huh? We're living in Uncle Pete's cabin in the middle of nowhere, and we don't even have money for a hamburger. That's an answer to prayer?"

"Please, Ethan."

"You know what, Mom? I try to pray. I do, and I don't get any answers—all I get is angry and confused. I'm angry that Dad just walked out on us, just like that. I'm angry that your so-called God let it happen. It just makes me sick."

Marietta Ware looked down at her son and reached for his hand. "But that's what anger does, Ethan. It will make you sick. It made your father sick. I tried to help him, to be a good wife to him. God knows I tried over the years. But he never stopped being angry. He only grew bitter with his hatred toward God. All I can do, all we can do, is pray for him—and try not to let the anger get us, too."

Ethan stood up and headed for the door. "I'm not going to do it. I'm never going to pray for that guy again. As far as I'm concerned, he might as well be dead."

TRAVIS THRASHER

Outside on the deck, away from his mother's gaze, the sixteen-year-old stood and wept bitterly. Tears fell again. Familiar tears. Tears he allowed no one else to see. Except for God, if there was a God.

Are you watching up there? Ethan asked, looking toward the heavens. *Can you see how horrible I feel, how sad Mom feels? Do you even care?* As usual, silence answered his prayers. That was the only answer he ever got: silence.

Leaning his elbows on the deck railing, Ethan struggled to regain control. He didn't want his mother seeing him break down. He needed to be a man now, something his father was incapable of doing. Ethan needed to be strong for his mom. He had no choice.

As he wiped his eyes, though, he thought he heard the voice of an angel. "Hello?" he said, looking up to the heavens. "Anybody there?"

"Down here," the angelic voice replied. It sounded familiar. Ethan looked below toward the road. There stood the petite, dark-haired girl who had showed up on the deck of the cabin yesterday. The same lovely girl he had thought about all night and most of this day so far. Sara Anthony.

"Talked with any groundhogs today?" Sara yelled up to him.

Quickly he swiped at his nose with a sleeve and cleared his throat. "Funny, 'cause you kinda sound like one," he replied, trying to sound as cheery as he had the day before.

"Very funny."

"You lost? Or decided to go trespassing again?"

"I just thought I'd come back this way. It's nice up here."

"You can come up to the deck," Ethan said. "I'm mostly harmless."

"Mostly?" Sara asked.

"Well, you're safe with me."

As Sara walked up to the deck, Ethan wiped his eyes again with the sleeves of his T-shirt. Thank goodness the road was far enough away from the deck that his tears could go unseen.

"Hello again," Sara said as she stepped out on the deck.

"Trespassing again," Ethan said with a smile. "You know, we might be forced to call the police."

"Very funny."

"So you can leave your camp just like that?"

"Well, we had some free time after lunch, and we're allowed to go anywhere between the church and the campground."

"Did you eat lunch? We've got every kind of Campbell's soup known to mankind."

Sara laughed. "Yes, I ate, but thanks. I enjoy the walk up here—the view is beautiful."

So are you, Ethan thought as he nodded.

They spent the next hour together, talking on the deck and walking along the road that wound away from the campsite and Ethan's home. Ethan wasn't sure why Sara had come back to see him, but he didn't think much of it. He only wanted to be with her—and to get away from the cabin, from the pain he had been feeling for a long time. He only briefly introduced his mother to Sara, avoiding any further conversation by telling his mom they were leaving. He would explain things later.

Their conversation was occasionally awkward, since neither knew the other. But Ethan was good at filling in any lapses when the conversation stalled. He kept making jokes, making her laugh every other minute. He enjoyed doing it. It was good to hear some laughter up on this mountain. There hadn't been a lot of it lately.

Around one-thirty, Sara told him she needed to return to camp. They sat on a fallen tree that overlooked the valley below. Ethan had found the tree one day while roaming the mountain. There weren't many things to do in the mountains beside roam.

"Maybe you'd like to come to one of our evening services sometime," Sara suggested. "I think it would be okay if we asked the camp director."

"Could I sit by you, or would they put me in the back row?" Ethan asked, joking as usual.

"Of course you could sit by me. I like sitting near the front so I can hear better."

"I don't know," he replied. "I'm not big into church services."

"It's not what you think. It's pretty casual. We sing and talk and the speakers are all great. You might like it."

"Well, you didn't mention anything about singing before!" Ethan sarcastically exclaimed.

"What, you like singing?"

Ethan laughed. "No."

"You'll still like it. I know you will. Come on."

Ethan doubted it but figured he could endure anything as long as Sara Anthony was by his side. "I guess I could try it out, see what it's like," he said. "What time is it?"

As Sara recited the time and place for the evening gathering, Ethan found himself lost in her dark, wide eyes. Soft and endearing, they gave her a look of grace he had never seen before. Strands of her shiny, black hair tended to stray into her eyes, and she would occasionally brush them back. He found it hard to breathe when she did that.

"Can I ask you something?"

Sara nodded.

"Why did you come back here today? I mean, I figured I acted like a total idiot yesterday and probably was rude on top of it."

"You weren't rude," she said softly.

"Well, then, just idiotic. Were you just walking by again?"

The corners of her mouth turned up slightly. "Why do you ask?"

Ethan shrugged. "Call me paranoid."

"The groundhogs sent me."

"Oh, they did?" Ethan replied. "Now I see. Are you the special interpreter they were talking about?"

"I am," Sara said with a shining smile.

"Oh, now it all makes sense."

But nothing made sense, Ethan thought. Nothing at all. Not his life, not his parents' marriage, not living on a mountain, nothing.

Looking into this girl's eyes makes sense, though, Ethan told himself. When he gazed into those eyes, for the first time in a long while he began to forget some of the pain he had been carrying around. All the anger and confusion simply seemed to vanish when Sara was around.

"I really do have to go back," Sara was saying as she stood up. "So, maybe I'll see you tonight?"

Ethan smiled. "Well, I will certainly have to check my calendar. I hear there is a big party in the woods tonight."

"Oh, really?"

"Sure. But, you know, I might have to miss it. I haven't been preached to for a long time."

"Nobody's going to be preaching to you," Sara replied.

"I might actually need some preaching to. Who knows?"

They had arrived at the cabin's driveway. Sara looked up at him and gave him another dazzling smile. "Are you ever serious?" she asked.

Ethan pretended to think a minute. "I'm afraid to tell you but . . . I really don't think so."

"Well, you'll have to behave tonight."

"It's a date," he said.

TRAVIS THRASHER

"A date?"

"No, not a 'date' date. You know what I—"

"Gotcha," Sara said, already starting down the bumpy dirt road.

Ethan waved and watched her go. He looked up at the cabin and suddenly noticed something amazing. The sinking feeling he usually got when he glanced at the cabin wasn't there.

Ethan remembered his own words earlier that morning as he had stood on the deck. They had been addressed to his mother's God. *Do you even care?*

Maybe, just maybe, God did care. . . .

Ethan pushed those thoughts away. Sara's appearance wasn't heaven-sent. It was just luck. Pure luck. Destiny. Chance. All those wonderfully curious things.

But a voice still turned over in his head.

Maybe.

There aren't enough words to describe my love for you.

goodbyes

"I WANT to take you somewhere," Ethan told Sara as they walked holding hands.

The final evening service had ended minutes earlier. It was the third service Ethan had attended in the last week. This one had started much later than the others so everyone could sit around a blazing campfire and listen to the pastor speak. He had held Sara's hand for the first time during the service. She had been hesitant when he first reached for her, but then she relaxed and let her fingers stay entwined with his.

Now Sara looked at her watch and shook her head. "I'll have to go in soon. I shouldn't."

"Come on. Break one rule. What are they going to do? Make you go home tomorrow?"

"Maybe they'll make me stay here," Sara said with a smirk.

"Now wouldn't that be a terrible thing?"

She gave in, so he led her up a hill that veered away from the campgrounds. Shining a flashlight before them to light the path, Ethan walked on through the dark woods. Sara silently clung to his firm grip. Ethan assured her it was safe. "I've been here a bunch of times," he said.

"At night?"

"Sure. That's the best time."

By the time they reached the big rock and climbed it, it was twenty minutes after curfew.

"I really have to go," Sara said in a nervous voice.

"I know, I know. But wait. Please. Just stay here for a minute. You've got to see this."

Ethan led her to the other side of the boulder. At the far edge, the ground dropped away suddenly, so that the giant rock seemed to hang far out over the valley below. In the distance, the silhouettes of hills and mountains stretched on forever. Two owls called back and forth to each other. Stars—millions of wondrous points—speckled the sky, lighting up the evening for them. And the moon smiled back at them from so close and far away.

Sara felt mesmerized by the majestic scene. Suddenly everything—the view, the mountaintop, Ethan—felt like a dream. "It's breathtaking," she uttered, instantly forgetting about the time.

She held on to his hand, and they both sat on the smooth top of the rock, talking quietly and gazing out at the sights below and above.

"I come out here and think about a lot of things," Ethan said. "I could never do that back home in Chicago. There wasn't anywhere to go."

"That's a benefit of living up here, isn't it?"

"Yeah, you're right. It is."

Sara knew about the ugly divorce Ethan's parents had just gone through. She knew he needed someone at this point in his life. And she was glad to be that person, if only for a few days.

"It's certainly peaceful," Sara said.

"I've been thinking about all that stuff they said at the services. I think that if I were to ever believe in a God above, it would have to be because of this."

"Because of what?" Sara asked.

"Because of this—this beauty. It's hard to believe that all of it just accidentally appeared one day."

Sara didn't say anything for a moment. She just stared off into the distance. "Then don't believe it was an accident," she finally stated. "It gives me hope to believe that God is above and that his plan included all of these mountains and stars and everything, including us."

"I think he might have goofed with me," Ethan said, half joking.

"I don't think he goofed. Not at all." Sara squeezed Ethan's hand.

Ethan nodded. "Did I tell you my mom believes in all that stuff?"

"She's a Christian?"

"Yeah, and she's always trying to get me to believe it all, too. It's just—I have a hard time. I mean, how can there be this loving God if life down here can be so horrible? When people are always leaving you, always saying goodbye—"

"God never leaves you," Sara said gently. "I look up above and know he is there, and sometimes he is the only one who keeps me secure and keeps me sane. I know he is with me all the time—like the day you first saw me."

"When you were praying?"

"Yes, when I was trespassing on your deck."

"I just—I don't know. My mom believes in all of that, yet how can she after my father left us on our own? I mean, she works so hard, and we can barely make ends meet."

Sara remained silent, holding his hand and listening. That was all she could do.

"Well, I know one thing I believe in," Ethan said. "I believe in us."

Sara looked at Ethan and smiled. His answering smile seemed as brilliant and as close as the light from the stars and the moon.

"I do too," she whispered.

"Can I ask you something, something serious, Sara? I actually want to be serious."

She nodded.

"I know this was weird luck, us meeting and everything. But I would really like to stay in touch. No commitments or anything, just stay in touch."

"We can," Sara replied with full sincerity in her voice.

"I know how these things go, when you meet someone and then you leave and go your separate ways. But right now I need to know there is someone I can believe in. Tell me you won't forget about me, about us."

"I won't. I won't ever."

Ethan moved toward Sara and gave her a sweet and simple kiss on her cheek. So brief and yet so meaningful, just like the last few days had been. Sara didn't move away; she looked back at him with a subdued smile.

"Sara, I've never met anyone like you. I know I'm young, that we're young, but I think I'm never going to meet anyone else like you. I don't want to."

Sara looked down. "I'm sorry," she said, wiping tears away. "I'm not upset. I just don't want to go. I don't want this to end."

"We'll see each other tomorrow," he said, but he knew they wouldn't have much time.

"Will you write me?" Sara asked.

He chuckled. "Remember? That's all I do around here besides talking with the groundhogs."

Sara smiled and wiped away more tears. "You will, then?"

"Of course I will," Ethan said. "But I want letters back."

She nodded. "It's a deal."

Ethan looked out over the valley below. "Wouldn't it be nice to spend the rest of our lives at a place like this, away from the world and its craziness?"

"I imagine heaven to be this beautiful," Sara said. "Even more."

Ethan looked into the skies and said nothing. Sara wasn't sure, but she thought he had tears in his eyes as well.

83 ≈ goodbyes

Your love gave me a chance.

letters

Dear Sara,

It's cold, and the holidays are almost here, and before Santa Claus kidnaps you, I wanted to say Merry Christmas. I miss you. Yes, two and a half years after waving goodbye to you in that van headed back to Tennessee, I still miss you. I write to you from the same apartment in Chicago. Snow is falling, and they're predicting something like a foot. I still wonder why so many people endure these Midwestern winters.

I hope your first semester of college went well. Mine—well, the junior college isn't much. I live at home and make the ten-minute drive every day. I work at a local supermarket in their—get this—"farmstand department."

Still writing—all the time, in fact. My social life—well, there isn't much of that. Mom hasn't been doing too well these days. I think it's this weather. She seems so tired and sick all the time. Besides going to a few classes and working and helping take care of the apartment, I write. Still trying to finish that Great American Novel.

Your last letter said you were pretty serious with another guy. Good for him. As for me, well, I still have this dream that at some point in my life, I'll see you again. I keep meeting girls and then comparing them to this dark-haired beauty I met years ago. I sometimes think nobody will ever measure up to you. I probably shouldn't do that, but I can't help it. You're special. I knew it the first time I saw you on the deck, praying of all things.

Thank you for the early Christmas present. The Bible is beautiful. I will do as you asked—I will read it. I promise.

Thanks for the photo as well. Needless to say, it is on my desk at home and is there in front of me whenever I write to you. The smile sends me off every day. Your sweet smile.

I hope the holidays and next semester will go well for you. Drop me a line when you can. I know you're busy. I'm still thinking about you.

Sincerely,
Ethan

Ethan:
Sorry for not having responded to all your letters. I love receiving them—I really do! The one you sent around Valentine's Day made me cry. Scottie and I broke up, and I felt pretty low, and then, of course, your letter and poem came. Thank you.

Probably the biggest thing in my life now is the news that my parents are moving to the Atlanta area. They'll be closer to me, since Covenant College is only half an hour from Atlanta, but still—I can't believe they'll be moving away from Tennessee. My dad is excited, and my mother's stressed—but she hopes to see me more. Sometimes that thought makes me happy, and sometimes it scares me to death. My mom and I have a, well, sort of a complicated relationship.

Sophomore year has been a lot more difficult. I'm taking a lot of basic courses that I have to take—like chemistry and philosophy. They're a lot of hard work. School's okay, but I think it'll be more fun once I get more into my major. I've decided to call it quits with the guys around here. I seem to do that every few years. Maybe if I meet someone who sends me poems and writes me lovely letters that will change. But I doubt it will.

I would love to see you. It's been so long—it would be hard to know how to act around you. I shouldn't feel that way, but I do. It seems like I know you so well. I mean, I guess I do, with all your letters and everything. They mean more to me than you'll ever know.

I pray for you every day. I still do. I pray for your mom, too. I hope she gets better. I'm sorry for all the stuff you are having to deal with. You have a huge heart, Ethan, and God certainly has plans for you. I know that.

I look forward to hearing from you. Take care of your mom and yourself.

Love,
Sara

*I think I can actually begin
to understand that love.*

surprises

SARA HEARD the fifth ring and stood up from her desk to answer it. She had assumed one of her four roommates was around. She roamed the suite to find the cordless phone, finally spotting it on top of the microwave in the kitchen.

"Hello?" Silence for a second. Annoyed, Sara said hello again.

"Sara?"

"Yes, this is she." Sara began to think this was either a sales call or a freshman prank. "Who is this?"

"Sara, it's Ethan."

She couldn't believe it. His voice sounded so different, so much older. For a minute she was unsure what to say.

"I'm sorry to be calling you," Ethan said. "It's just, well, I had to."

"It's okay. It's great to hear from you."

It had been more than a year since Sara had last heard from Ethan. He had called her only a handful of times since their first meeting. Ethan had always made it clear that he wanted to talk to her but didn't want to pressure her in the slightest way. Most of the time, the letters had been enough for both of them—for some reason they cherished the special quality of their written correspondence. But special circumstances, like the news of her family's move to Atlanta, had prompted him to call her. Even then, he always apologized for calling and kept the conversations short—just long enough to make sure she was doing okay.

This time he quickly avoided any pleasantries. "My mom is really sick," Ethan said, his voice serious and direct.

"Is she—is she okay? I mean, what happened?"

Ethan's letters over the years had detailed his mother's declining health. She had a rare disease that had only been diagnosed in the past year. Since then, she had stopped working. Ethan's letters had been optimistic, however. This call came as a surprise.

"I've taken her to get some tests and stuff done."

"Where are you?"

"Well, actually, that's why I'm calling. We're seeing a specialist at Emory University Hospital. My mother got a bunch of information on this doctor off the Web, and we decided to give her a try."

"You're in Atlanta?" Sara asked, surprised that he was only thirty minutes away from her.

"Yeah. I know this is a surprise and all that, but I'm going to be around for a while, and I figured—"

"Ethan, I would love to see you."

"I know I'm sorta intruding. You might have plans and all that—"

"No, of course not. Please. I could come up to the city."

"Or I could come see you."

"Well, if that's what you want," Sara replied.

"To be honest, that's about the only thing I want right now. I've gotta get out of this hospital. My mom will be resting and having more tests. I can get away tonight."

"Well, I was just studying."

"You sure are a party animal."

"Here, let me tell you the directions. We can meet at the college."

As Sara dictated the turns and landmarks, her body felt alive with excitement and worry. How did she look? Oh, she looked horrible. She would have to change her clothes and definitely do something with her hair, and—

"Sara?" Ethan said.

"Yes?"

"Look, don't worry about me coming. I know this is unexpected. I don't want to make your life—or mine—any more complicated. I just need to see you. Right now, I kinda need a friend."

Sara smiled and wished he was already there. "Just hurry and get out here."

Sara sat at a picnic table in the center of the campus lawn that stood between the campus parking lot and one of her old dorms, Alabaster Hall. The April evening felt cool and still. She looked up through the trees and saw stars and remembered the evening with Ethan on the mountaintop in North Carolina. Her heart raced at the thought of seeing him again.

When the figure came walking toward the dorms, Sara knew it had to be Ethan. He was taller now, but with the same thick hair and bouncy walk. He wore khaki pants and a polo shirt. When he got closer, Sara could make out the serious look on his handsome face.

"Ethan . . . ," she said tentatively as she rose and approached him.

He glanced her way, and his face changed. He smiled and walked toward her. "Is that really you?" he asked, standing before her and continuing to smile.

"It is," she said, unsure what to do.

He looked down at her and took her hand. "I've rehearsed maybe a hundred times what I would do if I saw you again. What I would say." He looked at her hand. "I've missed you so much.

I would have missed you more if I had known how beautiful you've become."

"Ethan—," Sara said, embarrassed.

Then Ethan let go of her hand and put his arms around her. She embraced him and buried herself in his open arms and against his chest. They held on to one another for several minutes. Sara realized Ethan was crying.

He pulled away from her and choked out a laugh. "I'm sorry. All that rehearsing, and what do I do? I act like a five-year-old."

"It's okay," she told him. "Things are going to be okay."

"It's so good to be near you again."

They walked over to the picnic table and sat down.

"It's been awhile, hasn't it?" Ethan said, once again under control, once again smiling.

"A very long time. Almost six years."

"Sorry to drop in out of the blue."

"I'm sorry to hear about your mother."

They talked for hours, first at the picnic table, then at a coffee shop, then in the living room of her shared apartment—about Ethan's mother, about each other, about their senior year at college, about their prospective careers, and about everything else they could think of. Sara remembered why she had fallen for Ethan. He had this gift of opening up to her and letting her see everything about him, even his insecurities. He talked about his mother, and she winced to see the pain in his eyes. She remembered the last time she had seen him—that summer when they met. The pain had been there then, too, from his parents' divorce.

Why does life have to be so hard for some people? she wondered. She felt almost guilty. Except for the occasional conflict with her mother on the subject of her future, her life was really pretty easy.

TRAVIS THRASHER

Before he left to go back to Atlanta, Ethan made a request of Sara. "My mother asked me to ask you. Would you go see her?"

Sara swallowed and nodded. "Of course. Now?"

"No, in the next day or two. I told her I would ask you, but please, don't feel like you have to. It's just—I know you guys only met the week of camp years ago, but I've talked about you so much, she feels she knows you."

"Ethan, I'd love to see your mother. I feel like I know her, too."

"Tomorrow, then."

A silence drifted over their conversation for the first time since Ethan had approached Sara. She could tell he was lost in something, holding back his thoughts.

"What are you thinking about?" Sara asked.

"I didn't even ask you if you had a boyfriend or anything. I know you said in your last letter you didn't, but . . ."

"I still don't. Ever since sophomore year. And it drives my mother nuts. Every time I talk to her, she asks me if I've gone on any dates recently. And I always tell her no."

"Why haven't you?"

"I don't know. There have been some nice guys around here. I just—I don't know. It seems the only reason I'd be going out with any of those guys would be to please my mom. That's not a very good reason, is it?"

"Probably not."

"And you? What about you?"

Ethan smiled. "I still think of you every day, Sara. Don't say anything, please. I just want you to know that. My letters, the stuff I pour into them, are all true. You probably think I'm an idiot for continuing to write so much to you—"

"But I don't. I love your letters. I just wish I were better at answering."

97 ≈ surprises

"Can I ask you one question, then? Just one?"

"You can ask me anything," Sara said, afraid of what he would say.

"Was the thing that happened in the mountains years ago—was that just some high school crush?"

Sara looked at him and shook her head. "No, of course not."

Ethan took her hand and kissed it. "Thank you so much for seeing me tonight. And for going to see my mom tomorrow. I promise, no more questions about us. For now."

The hospital room where Marietta Ware lay was warm and comfortable. Ethan had brought some things from home to make the stay a little more pleasant—a few framed photographs, a whimsical stuffed bear, and a compact disc player. Sara greeted Ethan's mother with a bouquet of flowers.

The woman lying in bed with a hospital gown on and an IV in her arm smiled as if Sara were bringing her flowers at home. "It's good to see you again, Sara. It's been a long time, hasn't it?"

After a few minutes of small talk, Marietta turned to Ethan. "Now, Ethan, if you don't mind, I'd like to have a few minutes alone with Sara."

Ethan looked at his mother with surprise, his face flushing a bit. "What for? Why do I need to leave?"

"I just have something I'd like to talk to Sara about, if that's all right."

"Mom, come on. There's no reason—"

"It's okay, Ethan," Sara said, touching his arm. "I'd love to talk to your mom. It's fine."

Ethan looked at his mother as if to warn her not to say anything she shouldn't. Marietta only smiled at her son as he left the room and closed the door behind him.

"Sit down, please."

Sara pulled up a chair close to the bed.

"You're all he ever talks about—did you know that? Or thinks about."

This time, it was Sara who blushed. She didn't say anything.

"I see all those letters he sends. I knew it years ago after you left—how much in love he was with you."

Love, Sara thought. He had never said the word *love.* Did he love her? Was that true?

"I don't really know you, Sara, except for the things Ethan has told me about you. But I do know you've been a positive influence on him. He has been reading that Bible you sent to him a few years back."

"Oh, I'm so glad. I thought it might be good, you know, with the questions he has."

Marietta Ware sighed. "I no longer try to tell Ethan what he should or shouldn't believe in. I don't have the energy to try and make him believe anything. Besides, he's an adult now. He's twenty-two, you know? I imagine you are, too. Anyway, he doesn't listen to me. But he listens to you."

Sara nodded, surprised by Marietta's words. She felt afraid of what the woman might say next.

"Can I ask you a question?" Marietta said.

Sara nodded at the gaunt and pale figure in the bed.

"Do you love my son?"

Sara breathed in deeply and felt herself blush again. She hadn't expected any of this. "Well, I-I'm not sure. I—"

Marietta grinned. "I'm asking for my sake, not for his. And trust me, this is just between us. Now, can you see yourself ever loving Ethan?"

99 ≈ surprises

"Well, of course. It's just—I've never said that. We've never used that word, but—"

"Ethan loves you, dear. He loves you more than his own life. I see it. I don't need to hear it to know."

"Mrs. Ware, don't misunderstand. I think Ethan is wonderful. I just don't know—"

"Sara, I'd like for you to make me a promise. Just hear me out, okay. Actually, I can't believe I am talking to you like this. If I knew I had another ten years to live, I wouldn't ever bring this up. But I think the Lord is calling my name, calling to bring me home. I don't have much time left."

Sara's heart sank.

"You know about Ethan's father and me, right?"

"Yes. I'm sorry."

"I am too. That's been the most heartbreaking thing I ever had to go through. And to see Ethan hurt. But it was my fault as much as his father's. I married him knowing full well he wasn't a believer and never wanted to be one. I thought I could win him over. But I-I learned that some people in this world will never be won over. They'll never know the truth. Or at least they can't hear it from someone they're married to."

Marietta pointed to the door. "Now, Ethan out there—I pray for him every day. I guess you might be praying for him, too."

"I do. Every day."

The woman smiled. "That's good to hear. We need to pray. Now, like I said, I need you to promise me something."

Sarah nodded. "What is it?"

"Regardless of what happens between Ethan and you, don't ever give up on him. You're my only hope, I feel. Don't stop praying. I'm scared that if I'm no longer around, he will grow even more despondent."

TRAVIS THRASHER

"Don't say things like that," Sara replied.

"Please, Sara, promise me. Promise me you won't give up on him, that you'll keep him in your prayers. He's so close, I feel. So close to knowing the truth. He needs someone to help him find the truth."

"I won't give up on him. I've always hoped that he would come to know the Lord. Then things between us would make more sense. Or at least make more sense to me."

"He has cursed God, Sara. I've heard him do so. The bitterness inside him has grown over the years. And when I'm gone, I'm afraid the bitterness will grow even more."

"I won't stop praying for him. I promise."

Marietta smiled softly and seemed to sink back into her pillows. She was quiet a few seconds, as if gathering her energy again. "There's one more thing I want you to promise," she said.

"What is it?"

"This may be hard," the woman warned.

"Just tell me."

"If he doesn't, if he won't—oh, Sara, this is so difficult. I want you to pray for Ethan. I want you to care about him. But Sara, you need to hear this. Don't let yourself make the same mistake I made. Don't marry a man who doesn't love the Lord—even if it's my Ethan. It'll only cause more heartbreak."

Sara squirmed in her chair. "Mrs. Ware, we're not—I mean, I don't think—"

Marietta looked at a picture of Ethan and herself on the bedside table. "I thought marrying the man of my dreams would make things easier. I thought that all we needed was love. I thought having Ethan would bring us closer. But in the end he left me. In the end, I realized I wasn't what he needed. It was Christ."

"I'm sorry," Sara said.

"I'm saying all of this simply to ask you to be careful. Ethan's the only son I have, and it would be a blessing for him to end up with a woman like you. But you have to be very careful."

"I will."

"I recently realized that the only things that will follow you into heaven are loved ones who trust in Christ. And to think of Ethan not being there—"

The woman stopped and breathed in deeply as she wiped her eyes. Sara held on to her hand and searched for the right words to say.

Marietta smiled and relaxed once more. "I'm sorry to drop all of this on you. Please don't think of me as some overbearing mother."

"You're like any mother—you love your son."

"He's a good kid."

"I know."

"And he really does care about you."

Sara nodded.

"Don't give up on him, Sara. And never give up on our Lord, either. He has a plan for all of us. That includes Ethan and you."

Is there a plan for Ethan and me, Lord? Will we have the chance to be together? Could we ever be together?

"I don't know," Sara said.

"The Lord knows, Sara. Remember that."

There is still so much to comprehend.

crossroads

ETHAN LOOKED out over the rocky ledge on the mountainside and spoke aloud to the emptiness he tried to convince himself he believed in.

"Will you take her from me, God?" he asked, the echo drifting away with the wind. "She's all I have now. You know that. How could you do that to me?"

He wanted an answer. He felt he had a right to one.

Is it too much to ask for?

The beauty answered him. The serenity of the skies replied to his words.

I need more, Ethan thought.

"God, don't take her."

He knew this was clichéd, his sitting on a hilltop, an unbeliever tossing up a last-minute prayer. But he didn't know anything more to do.

It had been a month since Ethan had brought his mother home to his uncle's cabin in Hartside, North Carolina. Every day he juggled the duties of a nurse, a maid, a cook, and most of all, a friend. He did everything he could for his mother. Yet nothing could stop the progression of her illness. Daily he saw her decline.

A week ago, Sara had driven up to the cabin to visit them. She had spent that week with them, sleeping upstairs in Ethan's loft room while he slept on the couch on the same floor as his mother. And in a way, despite his worry over his mother, it had been the best week of Ethan's life.

For the first time, Ethan was able to spend hours and days around Sara. He saw her messed-up hair and babylike complexion in the morning as he drank coffee; he got to see her eyes drifting closed as midnight approached. The two of them did everything Ethan had wanted them to do for years—watch movies they rented from the little store in town, take walks, talk for hours, read to each other from the various books in the cabin. It was more than romantic. Their time together had filled an emptiness in Ethan that he believed nothing else could.

But now that time was nearly over, and Sara would soon be leaving again. Ethan couldn't believe the week had passed so quickly, that he would have to tell her goodbye. *When I say that goodbye,* Ethan thought, *when will I see her again?*

He opened the spiral-bound notebook he had brought with him and began a short note for Sara to read after she left.

"What are you doing?" a voice asked from the forest behind him.

He smiled and closed the notebook. "Just writing," Ethan replied.

"I would have thought you'd want to see me some before I left."

"Do you have to leave today?"

"I've been here over a week," Sara said, sitting next to him. "I really should be leaving, even though I don't want to."

"Mom tell you where I went?"

"Yep," she replied with a smile.

"Strange how well your parents can know you, isn't it?"

Sara simply nodded and looked into the distance.

"What? What did I say?" Ethan asked.

"Nothing. Just the parent thing."

"What about it?"

"My parents don't know I'm up here."

"What did you tell them?"

"Nothing, actually. They think I'm still at college, tidying up things at the apartment before I go home."

"Will you tell them you came up here?"

Sara shook her head. "I don't know. I don't know what to tell them."

"Do they know about me?"

"A little. But with my parents, or at least with my mom, it's not that simple. She's got these . . . expectations. They expected me to meet some Mr. Wonderful at school and quickly get married."

"I'm not Mr. Wonderful?" Ethan asked, nudging her.

"Not their definition. They have such strong opinions about the guys I should date. My mom does, anyway."

He snorted. "I'll bet. And I bet a guy from Chicago who wants to be a writer just doesn't fit into what they think is right for their baby."

She didn't say anything. She just looked at him.

"But what about your expectations, Sara? You're an adult now. A college graduate. What do you want to do?"

"I just don't know anymore."

"Why not?"

"You're not listening to me. Things would be so much easier if—"

"If I believed the way you do, right? You want me to say there's a God. Okay. There's a God. I was actually just praying to him minutes ago."

"It's not that easy," Sara replied.

"Look, Sara, I know how deeply you believe in your God and all that stuff. And I wish I could believe it, too, but I can't. I'm not saying I don't believe in some of it, but all those rules and regulations, and this business with Jesus and the cross. I just don't know."

"I don't know either."

"What do you mean?" Ethan asked.

"I don't know about us."

"Sara—"

"No, I'm serious. Things are going too fast for me. I will start my first year as a teacher in a couple of months. I'll be living with my parents. There's so much going on right now."

"What about us?"

"This just complicates things, Ethan."

"Why? Tell me why it complicates things."

"Because you live in another state, for starters. And because we're so different. Not just in our beliefs. In everything."

"Just tell me this: Do you love me?"

"Ethan—"

"Do you? Answer me that question. Do you love me?"

"You don't understand. I know this is going to sound hokey, but there's no other way to put it. I love my Lord, the creator of everything in front of us and around us. And I just couldn't be with someone who doesn't share that love."

"Give me time."

"But how much time? Faith isn't something you can buy or something you can earn. You can't wake up one day and decide to have faith."

"So you're giving up on me."

"You know I won't do that."

"It's just, with everything going on with Mom and my life—"

"You need someone more than ever."

"I know I do."

Sara grabbed Ethan's hand. "Don't you see? I can't fill the void in your life. As much as you'd like to believe it, I can't be that person. The person you need is the same one who created this beautiful view in front of us. Remember that conversation we had here years ago?"

Ethan nodded and looked away.

"Can't you see that everything in your life is leading you into God's arms? Not mine, but his?"

Her words seemed to hang in the air. Finally he said, "Listen, let's not talk about this, not on your final day here."

"Ethan, we need to. I can't promise you what will happen when I go back home."

"It sounds like you've already made your decision."

Sara shook her head and stood. "Just keep reading that Bible I sent to you awhile ago. Will you do that for me?"

"Sure." Ethan rolled his eyes.

"I'm serious."

"Look, Sara, I know all those stories by heart. Noah and Moses and talking donkeys and all of it. My mom's been telling me about that stuff ever since I was little. . . ."

"Read the book of John," she persisted.

He gave an elaborate shrug. "Okay," he said. "I'll read it. Cross my heart and all that stuff."

"I need to get back to the cabin."

"Sara?"

She turned around and he stood, grabbing her hand.

"I know it takes a lot of guts to be honest with me. I know it's probably not easy."

She looked at him with sad, dark eyes. "And I appreciate your honesty. I know you could have just pretended to believe, and you wouldn't do that. But I just wish you understood what you're missing. The Lord fills you with hope when you're going through

rough times. He's always been there for me. I'm not making that up, either. It sounds like a line from a greeting card, but it's the absolute truth. And Ethan—you really need that hope."

Ethan shook his head.

"Keep reading that Bible I gave you," she said again.

He tore a sheet of paper from the spiral notebook he still held in his hand.

"Only if you'll promise to read this after you leave. It's something I wrote for you."

"It's a deal," Sara said.

What about our promises?

doubts

SARA DROVE for four hours until she couldn't take it anymore. Then she took the next exit off the freeway and pulled into a McDonald's parking lot. In the silence of her car she wept tears that seemed to bleed from her eyes.

Why, God? Why do I have to have feelings like this for someone who doesn't believe in you? Why did this have to happen?

She had hoped that the week's visit with Ethan and his mother would have proven eventful. She had dreamed of Ethan's praying with her and asking for God's grace and salvation. That would have been a dream come true. But instead, Ethan had seemed more defiant than ever. His resistance to God had seemed as strong as his desire for her.

What more could she do?

She unfolded the letter he had given to her.

Dear Sara:
Falling down and masked in silence
I mutter an insignificant farewell as you go
Driving into a sunset and a future
Realizing there's still so much of me you don't know
Seven days having passed so quickly
I still can't believe this goodbye has to come
I cloak my emotions into a chuckle and a farewell
My wisdom fails and the words come undone

But the memories, like the night, will never leave me
A star in the sky will link us together
And years and miles and forgotten moments might pass
But the fact that I love you will last forever

Ethan

He used the L-word. He actually said he loves me.

Sara folded the letter and laid it back on the seat beside her, then put the car in reverse and backed out of her parking slot. She felt weary and confused and unsure what to do anymore.

God, I don't understand why you have allowed me to fall in love with Ethan. I know I shouldn't be, so why does it seem so right? Give me an answer, Lord. Please give me something.

The miles of road stretched out before her. Every time Sara blinked, she could recall Ethan's melancholy smile. With every breath she took, she remembered the lostness of his eyes.

Be with him, Lord. Give him peace. Show him how much you love him, how much you love all of us. Show him the true meaning of the word he used in his letter.

Love.

PART 3

USA

Have you forgotten?

miles

ETHAN HAD DONE some stupid things in his life. In fact, he had done a lot of stupid things. He only hoped and prayed this wouldn't go on record as being one of them.

The speedometer in his '86 Honda CRX read seventy-five miles per hour. Ethan realized he was pushing it. One of the many questions he kept asking himself was, would his car endure the trip? He could picture it stalling on the edge of the interstate somewhere in the middle of Indiana.

Three weeks had passed since he had received the letter from Uncle Pete. On five separate occasions, Ethan had almost made the plane reservations for Germany. But ultimately he had decided to go with his gut feeling—to get in the car and drive and try to find Sara. What a hopeless romantic he was. Sara used to tell him that. But he knew it was one of the things she loved about him.

That was also where they differed. Sara would never just get up and go somewhere on a whim. She was so deliberate, so thoughtful and practical about every decision she made.

This certainly was anything but thoughtful—just getting in the car and driving to Georgia. Even though he didn't know where Sara lived, he knew her parents' address. He would spend a few days at his uncle's cabin in North Carolina before heading on to

Atlanta. Maybe a little time on the mountain would give him clarity regarding his trip to Europe. Did he really want to go?

Ethan remembered the late-night phone call he had made to Andy, his college roommate and buddy, not long before leaving Chicago. Andy had been delighted to hear from Ethan and asked when they could get together.

"We can't," Ethan had said. "Not now. I've got a dilemma on my hands."

Then he had explained to Andy about the decision he was weighing, about his desire to know for one final time whether or not he and Sara had a future. His old roommate knew the history of Ethan and Sara better than almost anyone; Ethan had told him the whole story many times in the past, over many beers.

"We should get together and talk," Andy urged.

But as much as Ethan wanted to see his friend, something told him that drowning his sorrows in more beer and sympathy was not the way to solve his problem. Not anymore. He turned down Andy's invitations. Several times.

Eventually, Andy told him what he wanted and needed to hear: Go find her then. Andy was a no-nonsense, "put up or shut up" sort of guy. That's what Ethan had always liked about him.

Ethan actually felt a bit of satisfaction at being able to tell his friend he couldn't see him. In the past, anytime there was trouble, Ethan had always tended to lose himself either in his writing or his few friends. Neither had made the problems of life go away.

But things were different now. He was different. Didn't Sara know that?

The old Honda felt unsteady. Anytime he approached speeds over seventy miles an hour, the car shook and threatened to break apart at the seams. And now it was loaded down with all his possessions—several suitcases and a couple of overstuffed boxes.

TRAVIS THRASHER

Taking off on road trips wasn't foreign to Ethan. During his wild college days there had been several weeks when he and his buddies went driving around the country, usually doing nothing worth mentioning. After college, just after his mother's death, he had taken off on a solo trip, a trip to find the meaning of life and to search for himself.

That had been when the writing stopped. He had driven the same Honda and filled the backseat with journals and books, planning to write down thoughts and poems and impressions and perhaps even a novel. He had written nothing on the trip, however, and almost nothing in the years that followed, except for the required articles he handed in to the editor of his newspaper. Ethan was thankful he could produce material in order to earn a living. But he hadn't been able to write anything else.

The trip after college had started his long bout of writer's block. The trip also happened right after Sara said no to his proposal. Memories of that journey still haunted him.

Hopefully this trip would be different.

So much was different now, although writing continued to be a problem. At the same time, writing wasn't his top priority anymore. What he needed to figure out was what he was going to do with his life. At thirty years of age, Ethan was basically starting over again. It frightened him.

What if I do find Sara? he wondered. *What will I tell her? That I have no job and I can't write anymore? That I have no idea what I'm supposed to do with my life?*

He didn't care. All he wanted was to look into those healing eyes one more time and hear the truth once and for all. Why had she stopped loving him? That's all he wanted to know.

He drove on toward North Carolina with only a vague idea of what would happen next. For now, it seemed like the only logical

121 ≈ miles

thing to do. He needed to get away from Chicago, yet he wasn't ready to go to Europe and be bound to his uncle indefinitely. He definitely needed to see Sara.

Please let me find some answers, Ethan thought.

*Now I understand the things
you once described for me.*

hilltops

SARA was on the third playing of her favorite Enya CD as she took the exit that would take her to Hartside. The uplifting voice and soothing music helped to dispel the cloud that rested over Sara's mood. She had already been driving in her convertible for four hours; she figured she had a couple more to go.

What am I doing? Sara wasn't exactly sure. Maybe she just needed some time and space away from everyone and everything. But going to Hartside to try and find it? No, there was more to this trip.

Maybe he's there. But that was silly. Of course Ethan wouldn't be in Hartside. But still Sara longed to see those beautiful hills one more time in order to think about what she was doing. It was only July, but she knew that December would be there in a few blinks of an eye. And if she wasn't 100 percent sure about marrying Bruce, she didn't want to lead him on.

Weeks after Bruce's proposal, Sara still struggled with doubts. This trip would give her the answers she needed.

She hoped.

Enya was singing, "This is where I should be now," and Sara felt that the words confirmed the feelings in her heart. This is what she should be doing. Unplanned and spontaneous—so what? Ethan would have been proud.

Sara didn't feel guilty. She hadn't lied to her parents or to Bruce. She simply hadn't told them where she was going. In fact, only her friend Elyse knew where she was at the moment. But she would call her parents tonight and tell them the truth. And the truth was simple: She wanted to go back to Hartside. To take a mini-vacation and enjoy her summer break. She didn't plan on being away for long—maybe just a couple of nights.

A week ago she had even discussed with her parents and Bruce the possibility of her taking a trip like this by herself. The general consensus was that they would all take a trip somewhere this summer. But Sara had nixed that idea without a further thought. She didn't want to go "somewhere." She wanted to go back to Hartside. And she couldn't bear the thought of going back there with her parents or, even worse, with Bruce.

Sara hadn't mentioned Hartside to her parents then. Her mother would have seen through her intentions. Her mother would have remembered the boy who once sent dozens of letters with a Hartside return address written on the envelope.

Like the highway that cut through rolling hills on each side, recollections of her past seemed to roll on and on. Light plumes of memory drifted across her mind. As she neared the mountain getaway, those reflections became clearer.

She was remembering the week she had spent with Ethan and his mother in Hartside after college. The week when Sara had realized she was truly falling in love with him, when he had told her for the first time that he loved her.

It had been only months before Ethan's mother passed away. Things had been so different then. For a while after that trip, Sara had even started to believe that Ethan was changing. He continued to raise questions with her in his letters, mentioned that he was going to Hartside Bible Church with his mother, and even admitted he had actually prayed for his mother's health. Sara continued to write to Ethan about how much she loved her Savior and what her faith meant to her. And Ethan seemed to begin to understand. At least Sara had thought so.

But then his mother died.

And everything changed.

It all seemed just like yesterday. With the music softly playing and the midday highway mostly empty, Sara continued to remember all the circumstances that led to their final farewell. Ultimately, she knew this was why she was going back to Hartside. To remember.

And what if I saw him today? Sara asked herself. *What would I tell him? What would I say if he asked how passionate my love for the Lord is now? Would I be as bold and brave in my response as I once was?*

The very thought brought a dread over Sara. She searched her motives and her feelings and tried to pray but felt the distance again. Maybe she was disobeying God by not putting enough trust in him. Maybe his will was so obvious and she was running in the opposite direction.

Sara thought of the passages in the book of Psalms she had read this morning:

"O Lord, you have examined my heart and know everything about me."

What do you see inside?

"O Lord, God of my salvation, I have cried out to you day and night. Now hear my prayer; listen to my cry."

Have you listened, Father? Have you heard me at all?

"Give thanks to the Lord, for he is good!"

I can't give him thanks. I am unable to. I know I should praise him in all things, but I just can't. I feel overwhelmed.

"For I am overwhelmed, and you alone know the way I should turn."

But it's so hard to keep heading in the right direction, Lord. I've had my faults and failures, but I've always trusted you like a child, Lord. All my life I've trusted and loved you, and yet why can't I have this one thing?

The Psalms continued to echo through Sara's thoughts. The words of David were always antidotes to sorrow, uplifting praises during life's heartaches. She knew the verses by heart and carried them close to her soul. But now she wasn't sure if they were more comforting or scolding.

"Have mercy on me, O God, because of your unfailing love."

I pray to see you again,
perhaps for just a moment.

miracles

THE MOUNTAINS felt like home to Ethan. He always felt safe in their rugged sanctuary. While he had spent many months in them over the years, they stood out for two memorable periods in his life: the time after his father left them, when he and his mother spent an entire summer in Hartside; and the time after his mother passed away, when Ethan had retreated to the solitude of the cabin. Where Sara had visited briefly . . . and left for good.

The latter had happened eight summers ago. *Can Mom be gone that long?* Ethan wondered as he sat on a rocking chair on the cabin deck. Eight years.

What have I done in those eight years? Ethan thought. W*ould Mom be proud?*

He didn't know. He didn't think she would have been proud. And this was the most haunting and hurting realization of his life. His mother had always wanted the best for him, and, growing up, Ethan had expected the best of himself. Dreams of being a writer, of finding the perfect place to live, of marrying the right woman— these had been normal for him when his mother was still alive. But everything had died when she did.

Everything except his love for Sara.

Ethan thought about writing to her again. Why couldn't he just give up and move on like any rational human being? When she didn't answer his last letter, surely he should have gotten the picture. For some reason, Sara was not a part of his life anymore. When she said goodbye all those years ago on the mountain, she really must have meant goodbye.

What will I say to her if I find her? Ethan wondered. He had never officially met her parents, so he would have to do some explaining to them. They might not be friendly, or they might not want to tell him where she lived.

But still he needed to know. He needed to be sure. *Just one more goodbye,* he thought. *One more goodbye is all I need.*

The midday sun warmed him as he sat there on the deck. The air was still and silent—almost too silent. Ethan stood up and stretched, then headed down the steps to the driveway. He would go into the town of Hartside to have some lunch. It might be good to go out in public and be around some other people.

It was around two in the afternoon when it happened.

He had just finished lunch at the downtown diner and was sitting in his car, wondering what to do next. The two-door Honda was nestled among a line of cars parked along the sidewalk. He was debating about whether to drive around or go back to the cabin when he saw her—and froze.

Could it be? No, surely not.

The woman walked casually by his car and along the small main street, stopping in front of the tiny bridal shop called Cherished Memories. He sat transfixed in his car seat and just watched her as she disappeared inside the store.

It was remarkable. She was stunning; he would have gawked at her regardless of whom she looked like. But the resemblance made everything in him stop, including his heartbeat.

TRAVIS THRASHER

Time and painful memories were getting to him. He knew they were. They had to be. The woman looked like an older and more beautiful Sara Anthony.

Impossible.

Never did he once consider that it might indeed be her. Things like that only happened in the movies. This was reality—dull, boring, normal reality. Painful reality. This wasn't the Jimmy Stewart movie in which George Bailey wakes up and realizes the whole town has just saved his life by giving him a boatload of money on Christmas Eve.

It can't be that wonderful of a life. No way.

The woman had short, black hair with long bangs that fell into her face. Her outfit was dressy casual—khaki pants and a dark shirt with a khaki vest. He couldn't see her eyes because of her black sunglasses, but still, the resemblance was incredible. The high cheekbones, the graceful walk, the way her hand brushed the hair out of her face.

You're seeing things now, Ethan told himself. *The cabin and this town are getting to you.*

For a few minutes he sat with his mouth half open and his eyes riveted on the door to Cherished Memories. Then he shook his head and looked around, trying to make sense of what had just happened. Nothing came to him.

He waited. His heart ached, and his stomach felt like it might either explode or implode. His brain thought a million different thoughts.

What if? What if it was her—sweet and precious and wonderful Sara Anthony? Would she look like that now, so sophisticated and grown up? This woman was almost intimidating; she couldn't be the same bashful girl I met years ago. Could she have grown up to be such an amazing-looking woman?

133 ≋ **miracles**

Cherished Memories. It was the same store they had browsed through years earlier, during that wonderful week she had stayed with him and his mother.

So what now? What was this woman who looked like Sara doing in that store? The woman emerged from the bridal shop forty minutes later. In the instant before she put on the sunglasses, her eyes gave him the answer.

It *was* her. It had to be her. Sara Anthony was standing there only fifty yards away from him. The love of his life was there, right there, right in front of him.

All the memories and the driving and the hopes and desires— and there she was, just walking past him on a normal street.

Wake up, George Bailey. It sure is a wonderful life.

He watched the woman walk to a shiny, late-model convertible, maneuver into the front seat, and drive off. And without thinking, not even sure what to think, Ethan followed her.

For thirty minutes he followed her around the town. It was as if he was following himself a day ago, when he had just driven up and down the streets, looking around. He felt like an idiot, following this woman. If it indeed was Sara, why didn't he just stop her? Perhaps run to her car and declare his love to her right away? He could easily flag her down and talk. So why didn't he?

He told himself he wasn't sure this was her. But even if it was, what then? What about his last letter, about everything?

Doubt plagued him. Once again, he was a fifth grader, too shy to talk to a pretty classmate, too embarrassed and insecure to see her response. But he knew this was Sara. It had to be. So why was she in town? Did she live here? No, of course not. Her car had Georgia license plates on it.

So why was she visiting the bridal store?

This was crazy. Insane. Ridiculous. Ethan shouted out thoughts to himself. "I'm nuts," he yelled out loud, trying to see if this was indeed a dream. It wasn't.

So what now? Only hours earlier he had been hoping, searching for some sort of direction as to what he should do about Sara. Now there she was in front of him, and he still didn't know what to do.

Her convertible ended up at a bed-and-breakfast on the outskirts of town. Ethan watched Sara get out and go inside, her short hair bouncing as she walked. He couldn't believe he was actually watching the striking figure in person rather than looking at a worn and outdated photo.

He started to pull over as he passed the bed-and-breakfast.

Go see her. Go see her now. Go to her, fool.

Yet he drove off back toward the center of town. He parked and walked over to Cherished Memories. He could feel his heart pounding and his breath quivering unsteadily.

Inside the quaint store, things hadn't changed much from what he remembered. Peaceful music played, the scent of roses hovered in the air, and everything was white and pink. Rows of dresses lined the walls of the small shop. The older woman at the counter might have been there years ago when they visited; Ethan wasn't sure.

"Good afternoon," she said with a smile.

"Uh, hi there. I was wondering. I saw an old friend in here earlier—or someone I think is an old friend. And I was wondering if you might have gotten her name."

The older woman looked puzzled. *Well, that's it,* Ethan told himself. *I really have gone lovesick and insane. I'm seeing visions now.*

"Lots of ladies come in. Could you describe her?"

So Ethan described the love of his life. "She's fairly short, nicely dressed, dark hair, wearing a khaki vest—"

"Oh yes, the elegant young lady. Very attractive."

"Yes."

"Well, let's see here. She didn't tell me her name, I don't think. I asked if she was visiting, and she said yes. I think she said she was from . . . let's see . . ."

Ethan didn't breathe for a second or a minute or an eternity as he waited to hear. The woman behind the counter remembered.

"She was from Atlanta. Or the area around Atlanta—that's right. You'd be surprised how many Atlanta folks we get way up here."

Ethan gulped in a breath of air and felt woozy. "Did she say anything else?" Ethan asked. "That she's married or anything like that?"

The older woman gave Ethan a puzzled look. "Are you from around here?"

"Well, yes and no. I mean, my uncle has a place up in the hills. Peter Madden."

"Oh, Pete? Yes, I think I remember him. So you're his nephew?"

"Uh, yes."

"I think I might have met your mother years ago."

"Maybe. Her name was Marietta."

"That's right," the older woman said, a smile on her face. "How's she doing these days?"

"She, uh, everything's fine." Ethan didn't want to go into details about his personal life, especially not now.

"The woman we were talking about, the one from Atlanta," Ethan said. "Did she mention anything about being married?"

"Well, actually, she said her wedding date is December 26. Odd date, wouldn't you say?"

He let out a surprised gasp. The woman from Atlanta part was fine, was good, was wonderful. But what was this part about marriage on December 26?

TRAVIS THRASHER

"Wedding date of . . . to whom? Can I, do you have the, uh, name?"

The woman looked at him for a second. "Are you okay, Son?"

"Yeah, sure, just real—I don't know—excited. I guess. A name or anything? Do you have one?"

"No. I'm sorry. She didn't talk too much. She bought a picture frame, I believe, and a card."

"A picture frame and a card?" Ethan asked, shocked and delirious.

"Say, you look pale, Son."

And Ethan said no more. He forgot to even thank the older woman as he opened the door and stumbled outside into the hot and crumbling world.

December 26? The day after Christmas?

Ho, ho, ho.

Ethan stood on the sidewalk and stared at the Cherished Memories sign. *Cherished memories,* he thought. *Maybe that's all I'll ever be able to have with Sara.*

All this way, all these years, all the love, all the dreams, all the hopes and desires . . . for what? For this little piece of wonderful information—that Sara Anthony is going to marry somebody else a day after Christmas.

The sun made Ethan want to faint. The only other time he had felt this horrible was after seeing his mother close her eyes for one final time.

But then, at least, he had been able to brace himself for impact, like a passenger on a 747 plummeting to earth yet able to buckle in the seat belt and prepare for the crash.

This had been too sudden. This time he had been blindsided.

It's all over, Ethan said to himself as he got back in his car and wondered what to do now.

137 ≋ miracles

*There are so many things
I want to tell you.*

decisions

SARA HADN'T EATEN anything for a day and a half. She didn't consider herself to be fasting; food simply wasn't on her mind.

She had a decision to make. Actually, in her heart she knew she had already decided.

But having made the decision didn't take away the sense of disappointment she felt.

She knew she had been foolish to think something might happen simply because she was in Hartside. She had told herself that if something didn't intervene, some miracle or some kind of obstruction, she would go through with the wedding. And there had been no miracle that she could see—no clear word.

Yet here she was, in a guest room all alone, still thinking about Ethan. So maybe there had been an intervention after all. Maybe this sense of sad clarity about what she needed to do next was God's answer to her prayers.

But it wasn't exactly the answer she had hoped for.

She found herself wishing once again that Ethan had not stopped writing her. He had always been so good about keeping in touch and letting her know how he was doing. She had never understood why it suddenly stopped.

But maybe that had been her fault. Maybe her response to his proposal had been the final thing. Maybe her no had been the end.

When she first came to town a couple of days ago, Sara had driven out to the log cabin where she had first met Ethan. It had only proved to be a haunting reminder of the last time she'd seen him. The place looked empty and abandoned, the same way her heart felt when she saw it. She had only stayed around there for a few minutes. The place held too many painful reminders of the past.

Now, in the stillness of her guest room, Sara found her thoughts straying back to that cabin—and that last day they had shared together.

It had been the winter after his mother died. She had driven up to the cabin to see Ethan, who was still staying there. At the time, she wasn't sure what would happen. She only knew that their relationship over the years had intensified. What had begun as a summer romance had built into an enduring friendship then blossomed into real love.

But what would come next? Marriage? Of course, she had dreamed of marrying Ethan. But that was out of the question.

Marietta Ware had been right. She shouldn't go into a marriage knowing that the one thing they disagreed on happened to be the most important basis for a life together: God. She didn't want to spend her years with the man she loved trying to convince him about Jesus Christ and his never-failing love. She couldn't do that to herself—or to Ethan.

When she visited him on the mountain after Marietta's death, Sara had wondered whether Ethan's heart had changed. She had hoped this would be the case, but her hopes were not to be realized.

She had shown up at the cabin with a furious mountain storm on her heels. And immediately she had sensed that another storm had settled in Ethan's heart.

TRAVIS THRASHER

Although Ethan had welcomed her warmly enough, the change in him had been obvious. She hadn't seen or talked with him at length since his mother's funeral, and her first glimpse of him troubled her.

He had grown a beard and looked quite thin. He was still handsome; Ethan Ware would always look handsome. But he didn't look healthy or happy.

"I'm glad you came," Ethan told her, giving her a big hug. Then he broke down and cried in her arms.

And in the course of the few hours Sara spent with him, she learned much more about his past summer than he had written her—about his aimless wanderings through several western states, about his inability to write, about his pain and defiance. He said he believed in God now, but he also hated the God who killed his mother. His words startled Sara and pierced her heart.

"Please, Ethan, don't say that," she said, but he refused to stay quiet.

He blamed God for everything bad in his life—his parents' split, his mother's death, Sara's reluctance to be with him, his own miserable existence, his inability to write. He told her how unhappy he was, how miserable life was without her.

"It's not me that you need, Ethan," Sara told him. "It's Christ and his love."

But he couldn't hear her. Or he wouldn't hear her. They talked for hours while the storm outside the cabin worsened. Finally, Sara knew she needed to leave.

But before she did, out on the deck in the deepening gloom, a desperate and breaking man proposed to her. He begged her not to leave, begged her to marry him, insisted they could work things out.

And Sara had no choice. She had to say no, aware that this no

143 ≈ **decisions**

was perhaps a final one. It was the hardest thing she had ever done.

But before she left, they made their promises to one another. Promises.

She could still hear Ethan's choked voice saying the words that still hung heavy to her heart. "I promise you with everything I have and everything I am that my love for you will never die." And her solemn response. "I'm going to make a promise to you. I'm never giving up on you. Every night I'm going to pray that you find your place in this world, that you find hope." A place in this world.

Hope.

Promises offered up before goodbyes.

But what had happened to those promises? She had kept hers. Had Ethan kept his?

Look at the irony, Sara told herself. *You kept both promises. You continued to pray for him, and you continued to love him. And why did I say no? Would I still say no? Would I still turn him away?*

"Love the Lord your God with all your heart, all your soul, all your strength, and all your mind."

I do, Lord. I love you so much. And I want my husband to love you as much, or even more. How could I possibly be with someone who doesn't even claim to know your name?

It should be so simple. But her feelings weren't simple. And no matter how many years passed, Sara was unsure if she would ever get over those deep-rooted emotions. Yet she knew the decision she had made back then and the decision she was making now were the right ones.

She began to pray. She asked God for peace, asked to be shown the way. And gradually she felt the peace settle in her heart. In this small Appalachian town so far away from home, peace came.

She had to be doing the right thing. She must.

TRAVIS THRASHER

She prayed for Ethan, for his soul, for his life. She finally accepted that what they had had was over now. Finished. And the finality of that acceptance filled her with a deep sense of sadness. Perhaps she should have realized that months, years ago. But those promises they made had haunted her.

Promises.

She had kept her promise. If only Ethan could know.

She thought of her life back home in Georgia. Of her parents. Of Bruce. She prayed for them, too, and for the courage to do what she had to do next.

Maybe Ethan wouldn't know that she had kept that promise, but Bruce and her parents would.

*I won't dare ask again,
but I still wonder
what you will say.*

farewells

THE SUN creaking in on Ethan through the side window of his car woke him up. His back ached and his right arm that had been used as a pillow felt numb and lifeless. As he wiggled his arm to get the feeling into it again, he realized that he had fallen asleep watching the bed-and-breakfast where Sara Anthony was staying.

Yes, now I'm really going places in the world, he thought. *If she saw me now she'd think I was some wacko stalker.*

He still had not been able to go inside and knock on Sara's door. All night he had tried to get up the nerve to do it. But he couldn't. Now, early this morning, he still couldn't.

How could he do that to her? She didn't deserve that. And he didn't deserve her. He never had deserved her—her love, her steadfastness, her commitment. He couldn't just crash into her world now and destroy all her plans.

She had obviously made her decision. He couldn't try to change it.

Still, he needed to be sure. He needed and wanted to see her one more time, just once more. The certainty of her decision would help him bring closure to an unrealized dream. He could take this memory with him to wherever he might go. Wherever life, however hollow it might seem now, might lead him.

The morning was just beginning. He would wait—just as he had waited years ago for her to come to him.

Months after his mother's death, the sting of losing her had still felt fresh and sharp. As weeks dragged into months, he had gradually grown more despondent about life. First, he had taken the trip west, attempting to put the pain behind him, only to end up feeling more lost. Then he had stayed in his uncle's cabin and done nothing for days and weeks. It was only after a desperate plea to Sara that he got a chance to see her again.

That was when he proposed to her.

He should have never thought he deserved a girl like her. He didn't. But she wanted to be with him, even though she ultimately said no. Another no—and for the same reason she had always said no to him.

God.

Ethan remembered cursing God many days and nights, blaming him for every horrible thing that had happened to him. Part of him had always believed in God's existence. It was the idea of a loving God that he had problems with.

As far as he was able to see, God had brought nothing but pain and loss into his life. God didn't love him—couldn't love him. And so he hurled curses and blame up into skies that seemed empty and cold.

So when Sara left him after he proposed—well, that had been just another reason to blame God. And it had been so easy to do. It was easy to curse someone who didn't give you what you wanted, to point a finger at someone in a distant heaven and place the blame.

TRAVIS THRASHER

That had been the beginning of all the events that followed, all the changes.

But, even though he had shared this with Sara, why hadn't she responded?

Half a day passed. It was coming down to one more goodbye. One final farewell. Ethan followed Sara back to town, back to fate and destiny and happily ever after and the end of all his hopes.

It was nearly noon. He had been sitting in his car for what— twenty-four hours? Almost. He felt dirty and greasy and his breath was probably horrible and if she saw him now she would surely run away from him. The years had only enhanced her beauty, made her look sleeker and stronger. And he looked, well, pitiful and desperate. Probably even insane.

Who cares? a voice told him. *Go see her; don't let her go. Don't, Ethan. Don't let this opportunity pass. You'll never have another chance like this.*

The voice lingered.

Sara's white convertible turned onto the main street and drove past his own car. The top was down, and Ethan watched her carefully as she passed. Her silky black bangs were blowing in the breeze. She had no idea he was so close.

Now, Ethan. Do something now. Don't let her go. Not again. Not like this.

But he couldn't say or do anything. He couldn't bring himself to speak or yell or move. She belonged to another. She loved someone else. He had never had any place in her life—not then, and not now.

He never would.

151 ≋ farewells

Honk the horn, the voice continued to yell. *Follow her! Come on, do something!*

But the convertible just drove down the street and out of sight. Ethan sat in his hot car and felt his stomach muscles tighten and his jaw clench and his hands grip the steering wheel.

He braced himself for an impact. An impact harder than any he had ever experienced. Lost love. The finality of it would hit him soon enough.

This was it. His moment. His moment to chase after her, to snatch her up and drive off into the sunset with her.

But Ethan knew life didn't always serve up happy endings. Sara deserved happiness. She deserved a joyous ending, a wonderful life. And all he would do was upset her, make her worry. He couldn't do that. He wouldn't.

"I love you, Sara," his breaking voice said out loud, as though she might hear and turn around.

She will never hear, Ethan thought. This was why he had come back—to find out the truth. And this was the truth: He loved a woman he knew he couldn't have—a woman who loved another man.

He started the car and began the drive—he didn't know where. He just wanted to get far away from Hartside and from North Carolina and from the memory of Sara. He wanted to go home. But where was his home? He didn't have one.

He had thought—and hoped—that his place was still at her side. He had been wrong.

"Goodbye, Sara."

PART 4

Am I simply being foolish
to think so much about you?

confessions

SARA HELD Bruce's hand as he stared off into the lake in front of them. They had been sitting on the bench for a long hour.

"And the trip—did you see Ethan?"

"No," Sara replied. "He wasn't there."

"I just don't get this. One minute things are set in stone, and the next you're driving off to North Carolina to find an old boyfriend. And then you come back to tell me we're not getting married."

"I told you why, Bruce. I don't know what more to say except how sorry I am."

Sara had told Bruce everything. Everything. Now, there was a concept. This was a first for them—another reason she had decided to break off the engagement to Bruce.

I want the man I marry to be someone I can tell everything to, Sara had reasoned. *I want to be sure it's the right decision. I want to go into the marriage without any doubts. Sure, there might be fears, but no doubts. No doubts whatsoever of my love.*

Sara had told Bruce exactly that. Her feelings didn't match his. Her love for him—was it a genuine love? She didn't know. And until she did, she couldn't go through with the wedding.

For the last hour they had been talking. She had apologized as she gave him back his ring. He didn't cry or yell; instead, he tried to reason and bargain with her. He looked more puzzled than distraught.

"Please just keep the ring," he told her. "And think it over."

"I've already kept one ring, Bruce. I can't keep another."

"But—you need to think this through."

"I have thought things through, Bruce. That's why I went to North Carolina."

"To find a guy you had a crush on when you were a kid?" Bruce said, desperation slipping into his voice.

"You don't understand," Sara said, taking her hand away from his and shaking her head.

"Sara, look, I love you. I want to marry you. I'll wait for you if that's what you want me to do. That's okay. It's just—I thought you were ready."

"Maybe at one point, I thought I was, too. I wanted to be ready. But I found out I'm not."

"But all of our talk about finding a house and starting a family. . . ."

"Don't you see? I always thought I would have those things by the time I turned thirty. I got scared."

"And that's why you said yes? You didn't have any feelings for me at all?"

"No, that's not true. Bruce, I really like being with you, and I think you'll make some woman a great husband. It's just—I'm not that woman."

"I think you are."

Sara took his hand again and looked out over the lake. Ducks swam around in groups. A small boy was throwing out bread crumbs in their general direction, quickly drawing a feathered following. The sky was a perfect blue, and the late July afternoon was unusually cool for summertime in Georgia.

TRAVIS THRASHER

Sara sought for the right words to say. "Did you ever have a dream when you were a kid?" Sara asked him.

"Sure. Starting my business, being successful—that sort of thing."

"My dream was to find someone who made me laugh, who loved me unconditionally, who was everything I'd never be. But I always ended up meeting guys who let me down. Then I met Ethan unexpectedly, and he was the somebody I'd dreamed of. He continued to write to me and stay in touch even as I dated other guys and lived far away. He never gave up on me. And years ago I realized I had fallen in love with him."

"But you don't even know where this Ethan guy is. It's been so many years. How do you know he hasn't given up on you?"

"I don't. But that doesn't really change things between you and me."

"But you want to marry this guy, right? If you saw him, you'd say yes and live happily ever after?"

"No. The things that kept us apart are still real. But I feel the same love I did years ago when he proposed to me. I can't explain that. I thought it would have faded. I didn't realize that the love I had for Ethan never left me."

"I can't believe this."

"Bruce, I'm sorry. I don't mean to hurt you. I just couldn't go on like this. I couldn't hide this from you—not something this important. And I couldn't go through with marrying you when I felt this way about someone else."

"This is just totally unlike you, Sara. I'm just surprised."

"Falling for a guy like Ethan was unlike me, too."

There was an awkward silence. Sara once again apologized to Bruce.

"What did your parents say?" Bruce asked.

159 ≋ confessions

"I haven't told them yet."

Bruce smiled for the first time that afternoon—a wan, regretful smile.

"Your mom isn't exactly going to be happy."

"I know."

They talked for another half hour; then they walked away from the lake and back to Bruce's car. He stopped her before they drove away.

"Sara, I know I might have pushed a little too hard for this marriage. And I know I'm not like this Ethan guy—I mean, I can't write poetry and romantic love letters and stuff like that. I'm just—well, what you see is what you get. But I want you to know I still love you—and I'm not going anywhere. When you're through waiting for someone who's never going to show up, I'll be waiting."

"Bruce—"

"I'm serious. You don't have to keep my ring. But if you have second thoughts in a week, or a month, I'll still be here. And you don't have to say that I'm the greatest love of your life or anything like that. Just say you'll be my wife, and that'll be enough for me."

"Please—"

"That's all. I won't say any more."

The evening's conversation would be even more intense and emotional. Sara was eating dinner at her parents' house. After they finished the meal, she asked if they could talk.

"You didn't touch your food, Sara," her mother said. "Are you all right?"

"Yes."

"How's Bruce? Are things okay with you two?"

Instantly her mother had picked up on what was going on. And instantly her mother's own fears had become apparent. Something wrong with Sara? Something wrong with the blessed marriage-to-be?

"That's what I want to talk with you two about. Bruce and me."

So for the second time that day, Sara told someone what she was feeling in her heart—that she couldn't go through with the marriage. Daniel Anthony listened with compassion and understanding on his face; Lila Anthony's usually composed expression turned to wide-eyed dismay.

"What are you talking about—you have feelings for someone else?" she said through clenched teeth.

"Mom, I still love Ethan Ware."

Lila looked at her husband, then back at Sara. "Ethan? The same Ethan from years ago?"

"Yes. The guy I met in North Carolina."

"Have you been seeing him? What? Did he contact you or something?"

"No. And if he had, so what?"

"It's just—I thought you were with Bruce."

"Mom. I know you two didn't want me seeing a guy like Ethan. I guess as the years passed, I thought my feelings for him would evaporate. But they haven't. I still love him. And I just think it would be wrong to go through with marrying Bruce when I feel this way about Ethan."

"Sara Anthony, what can you possibly be thinking?" Her even voice held an edge of hysteria.

"Lila—," Daniel said to his wife.

"No," she snapped. "This—this can't be happening. Why, we've been planning this wedding for more than a month now, and Sara can't be backing out just because of some ridiculous high school crush."

161 ≈ confessions

"Mom—"

"Lila, stop it."

The room erupted into a crushing silence.

"I'm sorry," Sara's mom said after a minute, her voice cracking. "I didn't mean that."

"You meant it. And I don't blame you for thinking it was a ridiculous crush. But it wasn't, Mom. It was more."

"Did you talk with Bruce?"

"Yes," Sara told her father. She detailed the conversation, told how Bruce had acted like a gentleman and still believed that Sara would come back to him.

"I don't want to hurt him any more than I already have, Dad. But he isn't the one. I know it now. Maybe Ethan isn't, either. But I can't force myself to love someone."

"Sara, maybe you just need to sort things out."

"No, Mom. I have sorted them out—that's how I came to this decision. Mom, I do want to get married. I want to have a family. But I just haven't found the one yet."

Her mother looked angry. "How do you know Bruce isn't the one?"

"Because I can't bring myself to feel for Bruce anything like I felt for Ethan. The feelings simply don't compare."

"But Sara, you haven't heard from Ethan Ware in years. What good is dreaming about something that won't happen?"

"You don't know it won't happen," Daniel said calmly.

"Well, I just don't want you to get hurt," Lila said to her daughter.

"Mom, please trust me. I know what I'm doing. I'm not waiting on Ethan. But I know—I just know Bruce isn't the one."

Finally Lila stood up stiffly and excused herself. Sara could see the unshed tears sparkling in her mother's eyes.

Alone with her father, Sara began to cry as well. Daniel came over and sat beside Sara on the couch. "So you really love this Ethan character, huh?" he asked as he put his arm around her.

Sara nodded.

"Don't give up on him, then. You know, I loved your mom for a long time in high school before she finally gave in and decided to go out with me."

"Things are a little different with Ethan and me," Sara said, managing a smile.

"I know. But God works in amazing ways. Allowing a bore like me to end up with a dynamo like your mother—now that's a miracle."

"You're not a bore, Dad."

"Well, your mother and I are certainly opposites; we always have been. Maybe that was the problem with Bruce and you. The two of you were too similar."

"I didn't want to hurt him, Dad. I didn't want to hurt anyone."

"You made the right choice, Sara. It's better you realized this now than a year from now. So no more tears, okay?"

"Okay."

He gave her shoulders a quick, tender squeeze, then pushed himself to his feet. "Now, if you'll excuse me, I think I'll go find your mother. I have a feeling she can use a good laugh. And I can always do that when she's upset, you know? One look at this mug, and she'll be smiling." He said it with an exaggerated wiggle of his eyebrows that made Sara smile, too.

"Good luck, Dad," she said as he left the room. Then she sat quietly for a minute before lowering her head into her hands and praying. *Lord, please let me know if I've made the right decision . . . or the hugest mistake of my life. Show me, Lord. Please show me.*

So I'll just say goodbye again.

bridges

"WANT ANY MORE?"

Wiping the sweat off his forehead, Ethan looked over at the long-haired man who was offering the canteen and shook his head. "I'm good. Thanks."

Ethan sat on the edge of a low-incline roof, resting and enjoying the perfect July day. Jeff Richmond, whom Ethan had met only a week earlier, sat next to him and took a breather himself.

"Probably didn't think that meeting a neighbor would result in a bout of manual labor, huh?" Jeff asked, the wide grin on his face showing through his thick black beard.

"Actually, I was wondering about the last time I worked so hard. Kinda sad to admit I can't remember."

Jeff laughed. "Well, all I can say is I appreciate the help. And I know Mister and Miz Forrest will be grateful."

Ethan nodded. "Actually I'm having a good time. Like I told you earlier, it wasn't like my Thursday was packed with lots to do."

Since nine o'clock that morning, Ethan and Jeff and some other younger guys had used shovels and pitchforks to rip the shingles off the roof of the fifty-year-old cabin. The following day they would be putting up new tiles. Charlie and Rowena Forrest, the elderly couple who owned the cabin, had been living with a leaky roof since spring, but soon they would be enjoying drier quarters.

Enjoying the tranquility of the remote location, Ethan found it surprising that he was here. Not only on a rooftop working harder than he had in years, but still in North Carolina. Still staying at his uncle's cabin, only ten minutes away. Still walking the dirt roads of the rolling hills he was growing to love more than ever before. Still here long enough to meet neighbors like Jeff Richmond.

Ethan had seen Jeff on one of his afternoon walks. The good-natured man a few years older than Ethan had talked to him for over an hour, then invited him to dinner. After that, the two had seen each other every day, and Jeff had grown comfortable enough in their friendship to ask Ethan about this work project.

I was supposed to be in Germany. I was supposed to be working alongside Uncle Pete. But he was still in North Carolina, biding his time. *What am I waiting for? What do I really think is going to happen?*

"So, any more thoughts about that trip you're supposed to make?" said Jeff, reading Ethan's mind. "I hope this little job hasn't delayed anything."

"No," Ethan replied. "I wasn't really going anywhere. For a while I was thinking—I was convinced—that I knew what I was going to do. And if things didn't work out, then that was a sign that the trip was a go. But these days—well, I'm kind of thinking I should stay here."

"You're kidding! You mean, not go to Germany at all?"

"Is that crazy?"

"Well, I don't know," Jeff replied in his twangy mountain drawl. "I guess most folks'd jump at the chance to go to Europe and all that. But not me. I've lived around here most of my life, and it's been pretty good for me. I figure it doesn't matter where you live. It's what you end up doing."

TRAVIS THRASHER

"How long have you been helping out people like the Forrests? You do a lot of projects like this?"

"Guess so. No big deal, really. I've worked for the hardware store in town most of my life—that's because my daddy owns it. And he helps out on supplies and stuff for projects like this. Mostly I do things like this in the summer before winter comes and you can't do anything."

"I think it's admirable—helping people like that."

"The Forrests here—he's about eighty and she might be the same. They're right healthy for their ages, but it's been awhile since he could get up here on the roof. I figure that's why God made us younger guys strong—so we can help out with some of the physical stuff older folks can't do. It's not so much admirable. It's just doing what you can."

"Well, let's just say I haven't always gone out of my way to do what I can," Ethan replied.

Jeff pushed himself to his feet, balancing carefully on the cabin roof. "You could've told me no. You even had an excuse. Germany. To be honest, when you first told me about that, I thought you were making it up."

"I sometimes wish I was."

"You got somebody waiting for you in Germany?"

"No, that's the thing. I was hoping someone was waiting for me here in the States. Someone really special to me. Turns out I was too late."

"Sorry to hear about it."

Ethan stood and picked up his shovel. "People move on, you know. I guess we all have to. Maybe I should, too. It'll be hard to be around here this winter."

"What's happening in winter?"

"That someone I was talking about is getting married."

169 ≋ bridges

"Oh," Jeff said, nodding and putting on his gloves. "Well, you know what they say. Hard labor is good for heartache."

"They say that?"

"No. But it sounds good, huh?"

Hard labor is good for heartache. "Yeah, it does."

Ethan began ripping more chunks of tile off the rooftop, deliberately pushing thoughts of Germany and winter weddings and Sara out of his mind.

It was the start of a new beginning. A moving on. A bridge had been crossed, and he stood on the other side, not wanting to look back.

Turn around, Ethan, a voice whispered. *Turn around just one more time. Just one more.* Ethan ripped up another row of shingles and hurled them off the roof. *Nope,* he told himself, *it's time to move on.*

But something pulled at his shoulder and begged him to not give up. He shrugged off the thought and dug into the roof again. *I'm moving on. This is it.* Don't give up yet. Turn around. Go back over the bridge and make one more valiant attempt.

That's what I did coming back here. I made one valiant attempt. It just wasn't valiant enough.

Remember these words.

discoveries

IT'S A BRILLIANT SUMMER DAY at Hope Springs camp
*in Hartside, North Carolina. Ethan leads Sara through a golden
field, holding her hand. Bands of horses race by them, hooves pounding, but when they turn to watch, the animals are gone. She and
Ethan feel like children but they aren't; they're adults.*

*Ethan sits down in the middle of the field, and Sara sinks down
beside him. She looks at him and wonders why he has been so silent
so long. It's not like Ethan to be silent.*

"What are you thinking?" she asks.

*They had been laughing earlier. Ethan still knows how to say
things, crazy and bizarre things, that make her laugh. Sometimes she
would laugh so hard that her side ached. Now, only minutes later,
Ethan is serious.*

"I'm thinking of you," his voice says as he looks into her eyes.

"I hope they're good thoughts," she replies.

*"It's strange, you and I. I mean, how I can care so much about one
person, yet realize that we can't be together?"*

*Sara doesn't say anything. She only stares at the handsome man
beside her. He still resembles the kid she met years ago, but he's
bearded now and thin. Terribly thin. His eyes are so sad.*

*"I remember growing up," he continues, "and always meeting new
people and fascinating people and people I knew I could never get to*

know. Girls. So many girls. And for one reason or another, I always knew I would never get to know them. They were too stuck up or too shy or whatever. But you—"

"What?" Sara asks.

"You opened yourself up to me so many years ago. I got to see a side of you that made you even more charming, even more beautiful, than I ever thought or dreamed someone could be. And through the years of writing and all that, I grew to cherish that love. I grew to cherish you."

"Ethan," she begins, but he waves her off.

"Please. Let me finish. This might be the last time I ever get to say words to you."

"But you're here, beside me. What do you mean?"

"You know what I mean. I can never have you. We'll never spend a day together in a field alone without a care in the world."

"But we're in a field now," Sara protests.

But they aren't. They're in a hospital room, sitting on the edge of a bed. Someone else is in the room, but she cannot see who it is.

"I'll never be able to wake you up and kiss you on your cheek." Ethan is still talking, as if the scene had never changed. "I'll never be able to know what it's like to see you every Saturday morning, sipping your coffee and relaxing."

"Why can't you, Ethan?" She feels as wistful as he looks.

"Because you gave up on me, Sara. You gave up."

"Oh no I didn't. You don't understand."

Suddenly panicked, she reaches out her hand to him, but he's not there. He's standing on the deck of the cabin, balanced against the rail, leaning backward. She tries to walk toward him, but her feet feel frozen to the deck. His voice still echoes in her ears. "I'll hear your name two or four or ten years down the road and maybe I'll even see you. I'll still have these feelings. But I'll never be with you. . . ."

TRAVIS THRASHER

"Ethan, I want you to—"

"Goodbye."

Sara finds herself alone in the hospital-room bed, under stark fluo-rescent light and echoing silence. She feels the protest welling up in her like the cry of a little girl lost.

"But I don't want to say goodbye. . . ."

Sara awoke before being able to. She tried to fall back asleep in order to capture the dream again, thinking somehow that she could put everything right if she could just go back.

But it was no use. She was wide awake. The dream was gone.

She sat up in bed, hugging her knees in the cold room. She could still feel the sadness, the emptiness of that dreamed good-bye. But with it was an eerie calm, a strange sense that somehow, in spite of what had happened, all was well.

That was when it occurred to her that dreaming about a man she might never marry was still better than marrying a man she never dreamed about.

She rested her head on her knees as the dream began to fade away into daylight.

The chill of winter normally made summer and all its pleasant memories easy to forget. But Sara found it hard, even now—five days before Christmas and six days before what would have been her wedding day—to shake the memories of previous summers and to erase the pain of this past summer. She had felt a little better ever since school started; her kindergarten class of twenty-two kids was one of the best she'd ever taught. During the days, if she tried, she could lose herself in the world of fingerpaint and ABCs and put behind her the two chances at love she believed had passed her by.

175 ≋ discoveries

She had no regrets. She still believed she had made the right decision about Bruce.

The memory of Ethan was fading a little. Now she could go a day without thinking of him. During the summer it had been so hard, especially after reading his letters and looking at the photos and other keepsakes. But months ago, after leaving Hartside and breaking up with Bruce, she had told herself no more. The box with all its precious, meaningful contents was back in the bottom of her closet, untouched.

Yet thoughts of him still haunted her unguarded moments. Even when she deliberately forced herself to move on, to stop dwelling on something that would not happen, she would wake up as she had this morning after dreaming of him.

Why can't I just forget him?

It wasn't as if anything had changed. There had been no word—not a letter or a phone call or anything. She had no way of knowing where he was—or even if he was alive.

But it's okay, she said to herself. *It just wasn't meant to be. I put it in God's hands and this is what he wants. Yet I still want to see Ethan. Just one more time. Just to find out what happened . . .*

In an empty house on a rainy Monday morning—the first day of her Christmas vacation—Sara found that she couldn't shake these thoughts. She found herself thinking about Ethan and her dream, of his smile and his blue eyes. Of his infectious grin and the way he always made her laugh. She had always loved that about him.

She could surely use a good laugh now.

She thought of going to see her parents. Dad was working, and Mom had probably gone off to do some morning errands. Sara wondered when her relationship with her mother would improve. They were talking, and things on the surface seemed fine, but she knew her mother too well to trust the way things seemed. Sara's mother had been devastated by the breakup, and the only way she had been able to cope was by staying busy. Things like reorganizing the church soup kitchen and volunteering for the symphony guild and even trying out new hobbies like teddy-bear collecting.

Sara recalled one of her mother's latest purchases—a Paddington bear—and thought, *What's she doing with all of these bears? Trying to find the right one to marry me?*

The flip calendar on a side table reminded Sara of how close she had come to marrying the wrong one.

Thank you, Lord, she prayed again, a prayer she had grown used to praying.

Since breaking up with Bruce, she had seen him only a handful of times. Almost every time, he had tried to bargain with her, giving her reason after reason why she should marry him. He hadn't even seemed to care that Sara still loved Ethan. Her resistence had only seemed to harden his resolve.

Then, the last time she had spoken with Bruce, though, he had made it clear that his patience was wearing thin. "I'm older than you, Sara," he had said. "I can't wait around all my life."

Since then, Sara had seen him talking seriously with one of the younger women at their church. It didn't bother Sara at all. It simply confirmed her conviction that she wasn't ready to get married.

Not to Bruce, anyway. Sara stuffed that thought. She wasn't ready to get married. Period.

Hours later, after a light brunch of a toasted, buttered bagel and coffee, Sara drove out to see her mother. It was close to one o'clock, and Lila was still out. Sara let herself in with the key, made herself a cup of instant hot chocolate to chase away the damp chill, and went to the front to bring in the mail. Sara always enjoyed getting the first look at the variety of catalogs and magazines her mother received. Lila Anthony probably had about a dozen subscriptions to magazines like *Better Homes and Gardens* and *Southern Living*. Flipping through one of those would help Sara pass the time until her mother got home.

The handful of mail looked too large to examine there in the entranceway, so she carried it over to the little table against the wall. Idly she sorted through it. Bills, junk mail, a magazine for teddy-bear collectors (what next?), and a letter in a long envelope.

She laughed when she saw the bear magazine, then stopped when she saw the letter. It had her name and her parents' address on it.

A chill went through her as she looked at the return address. The letter was from Hartside, North Carolina. From the place in the hills.

The last place she ever saw Ethan Ware.

She opened the envelope and unfolded the letter. The handwriting was familiar. Even after so many years, it looked the same. She glanced at the bottom and saw the name: Ethan.

She inhaled sharply. When she felt the tears begin to flow, she folded the letter up again. Looking around, making sure that nobody was near, Sara carried the letter into the family room. She needed to sit in case she fainted or passed out. Her hands shook as she opened the letter again. With the back of one hand she wiped the tears away.

How long has it been, Ethan? Why all of a sudden are you writing? Why now?

Sara wanted to read the letter but also feared to, wondering what he might possibly say. Ethan, the man she had turned away but never given up on. Ethan, her first love, perhaps her only real love.

She took the words in carefully. It had been so very long.

TRAVIS THRASHER

My Dearest Sara,

For many months I have fought the urge to write you. But as I look on the calendar, I know it is almost time for your wedding. Today is December 14, so it is only twelve days away. Twelve days. The pit of my stomach still aches from knowing this, from knowing you're twelve days away from saying "I do" and spending the rest of your life with somebody else.

Somebody else—two words I have told myself over and over yet neither believe nor want to believe. I always believed you would be marrying me. Part of me foolishly still does.

You are surely wondering how I know. But before I explain, I need to ask why you never responded to my letter—the one I sent you last spring. Months ago I found out the truth—that you had fallen in love with somebody else—and that explained a lot. But the things I told you in that letter, the things I expressed to you in that letter—well, I always thought that you would be happy about that and write me back, even if you didn't love me the way you used to. I imagined so many times the words you might send. But no word from you ever came.

Perhaps you didn't want to write, or you couldn't write, or you didn't know what to say. I wish you could tell me. But now it is too late. I understand that. You have your life to live, and I understand that, too. But I need to tell you some things, some more things that my last letter didn't say.

You know I still love you with every inch of my heart and my soul. I began loving you under a star-filled sky one night as a teenager when I didn't realize how big the world could be and how impossible some dreams would be to achieve. My dreams— you know them all, Sara. You know each and every one because I've shared them with you and because you are in every one of them.

Over the years I have spent so much time simply dreaming. Dreaming about spending time with you and dreaming about what it would be like if our love was to work out. I've been good at dreaming—you know that. I guess perhaps my greatest and grandest dream of them all was that, in the end, I would be at your side. I would hold your hand and walk out of that church into a crowd of smiling and happy faces, and I would know that finally, finally, Sara Anthony belonged to me.

I will never stop dreaming this, nor will I ever stop loving you, Sara. You were the love of my life. You gave me a part of yourself I don't think I can ever return. And, most important, you pointed me toward something more important than any of my dreams. You showed me where to find the answers to all those questions I had. You allowed me to find something, to be given something I can never fully thank you for.

But I don't want to go into that again. Surely my last letter said it all. But know that everything I said is still true. I still believe in you and in us.

In case you're wondering how I found out about the wedding, this summer I went to Hartside and I saw you there and found out about your plans. Why our paths crossed then was, well, beyond me. I don't even understand why I didn't speak to you then. But I am learning that I don't always have to under-stand—that's where faith comes into the picture. Didn't you say that once?

Anyway, I saw you and wanted to say something and take you in my arms—oh, Sara, how I longed to just simply look into those shining eyes and see you smile and hear your wonder-ful laugh. But I let you go. I watched you drive away.

So why I was in Hartside doesn't really matter. I found what I was looking for—the truth. And the truth hurt.

I am writing to you days before I board a plane for Europe. I'm moving to Germany to work for my uncle—you know, the one who owns the cabin. Much has happened to me in these past few months. So much—oh, I wish I could tell you it all. I will be gone for a couple of years or maybe even more. Remem-ber my dream of traveling to Europe? Well, at least that will be coming true.

Oh, yes—one more thing I wanted to tell you: The words have come back to me. Remember, in my letter, I said they had left me? Well, seeing you in Hartside seems to have brought

*them back. So I am writing again. I have written so much
lately, it's like the words were stored up all this time.*

*Sara, you always have been and will continue to be my inspi-
ration. After five months or so I just finished writing a novel.
Well, a novella, really. It's about a young man searching for his
lost love. He never finds her—but that's how classics end, right?
Tragic? I guess we're destined to be a classic.*

*I wanted to say goodbye again. I've spent a lifetime telling
others goodbye, half a lifetime telling you goodbye. Wishing you
were by my side, but always realizing you couldn't be. Now, as I
leave to be away for a long time, and as you prepare to be married, I say what could be a final goodbye.*

*Know this: Know that my promise still remains. I haven't
stopped loving you, Sara. I will always love you. You will be in
my heart wherever I go.*

Thank you, Sara. Thank you for everything.
I love you.

Ethan

For half an hour Sara sat still, reading the letter again and again
and looking out the windows to the backyard and wondering why
this letter had reached her and questioning everything about her
life and fearing her own thoughts. The tears flowed, as so many
had in the last few months. Sara touched them and then laughed
when she realized they weren't tears of sadness.

She felt elated.

She read the letter again. It was true. He had kept his promise—
he still cared for her, perhaps more now than ever before. How
could that be? She didn't know, but she didn't need to know why.
The only thing that mattered was that he still loved her. He still
loved her.

And she knew she still loved him. She loved him beyond a
doubt.

181 ≋ discoveries

Yet he was leaving to go to Europe—for a couple of years, he had said. He believed she was still getting married.

Wasn't this where they had left things off years ago? He loved her so much, and she loved him so much. And they couldn't be together. So in a sense, nothing had changed.

Or had it?

What was that letter he kept mentioning? The "last letter." She hadn't received a letter from him in years. He had said he sent a letter in the springtime. She searched her memory for anything she might have received then. She was sure she had received no letter last spring.

If indeed he had written it—and of course he had; why would he lie?—what had he said? Would that letter have changed things?

She reread the new letter and realized that now, for better or worse, her life was going to change. It had to change. She needed to know if there would be—if there could be—a future with Ethan.

She thought for a minute on what to do.

She prayed for answers. "Father, please help me to know where to even begin with this. I feel helpless here."

Thoughts attacked her. Call him. But that was impossible. He had sent this letter from the cabin in the mountains, and the cabin had no phone. Besides, he had probably already left for Europe.

Try the Chicago number.

Better yet, go find him.

But that was foolish. Go where? She couldn't. She shouldn't. But she had to do something.

Still sitting on the couch, her eyes all teary and her face pale in shock, Sara heard the front door open.

"Sara?" her mother's voice called.

The footsteps came in, then stopped. Her mother looked at her with a smile frozen in horror, as if somebody had died. "Honey, what is wrong?" Her mother rushed to her side and sat next to her.

Sara shook her head and smiled, wiping away tears from her eyes.

"What happened?" her mom asked.

Sara picked up the letter and waved it. "I got this letter, Mom. It came in your mail addressed to me."

And as her mom looked in disbelief at the envelope, Sara suddenly felt a cold chill of understanding. Her mom didn't look surprised or bewildered; she looked angry.

"Mom—"

"Sara, he shouldn't be writing to you. Not after all that's happened."

"What are you talking about?"

"You said yourself that you had made the decision to move on—right, Sara?"

"What's that have to do with anything?"

"I just think it's unfair for this young man to continue to write to you and upset you."

"Mom, I'm not upset about the letter. It's the best thing that's happened to me all year." Sara thought for a minute, looked at the letter, then back at her mother. "Did Ethan send any other letters this year to this address? Mom?"

The initial silence answered her question. Sara stood up and backed away from her mother as the awful truth continued to wash over her. "Mom, answer me."

Lila Anthony looked grave and speechless. Brief tears filled her eyes, but she quickly wiped them away. She attempted a nervous smile. "Sara—"

"Mom, answer me now! Did you take a letter that was sent to

183 ≈ discoveries

me? Did you? Did you steal a letter from me and lie about it? Mom!"

"Yes, yes, I'm sorry, but, you don't understand—"

"What? What don't I understand? How you could have lied to me for so long?"

Sara could feel the anger building inside of her. She knew that if she stayed in this family room much longer she would say hateful things to her mother. She fought to control herself.

"I'm sorry," her mother was saying, "but—"

"But what?" Sara screamed.

"It was Bruce. He told me about his plans to propose to you this past spring. And I was so excited about that and for you. And then this letter came one day. It was from that Ethan, and—well, I always had a feeling about you and that boy. I was afraid if you started writing him again, that would just ruin everything. And well . . . I just took it."

"What? Mom! What were you thinking?"

"I don't know. I thought—I don't know what I thought. But he was never right for you. You said that yourself, Sara. You said you could never be with him."

"And that was my decision. Not yours. Not anybody's."

"I just thought—"

"You didn't think, Mom. You lied to me, and you stole what was mine. Where's the letter now? What did you do with it?"

Her mother's tears began coming again. She choked out her reply. "I threw it out. I'm so sorry."

Sara fought the tears and fought her anger. She needed to leave, to get out of this house and to be able to think and breathe. She headed toward the entryway to collect her purse and wrap. But she couldn't stop herself from saying more. "How could you do something like that to me? How?"

TRAVIS THRASHER

"Honey, I told you. Things between you and Bruce were going so well, and I thought the last thing you needed was to be confused. I didn't want you to be hurt any more than you already had been."

"What do you call this, Mom? You don't think this hurts me?"

"I'm sorry, Sara. I don't know what else to say."

Sara stared down at her mother. "You know, I've never understood what your problem was with me loving Ethan. You never liked me getting those letters, Mom. Never."

"Honey, I just didn't think he was the right one for you."

"But how do you know that? You never even met him. Besides, isn't that a decision you should leave up to me—especially now? Mom, I'm thirty years old. I can make up my own mind."

Lila Anthony remained silent on the couch, her face white and her eyes red.

Sara got her purse and put on her coat. Before leaving, she faced her mother.

"Ethan might not be the right one for me, Mom. But that's something I have to find out. You guys were so set on Bruce being the right one, but he wasn't. I just wish you'd stay out of my life when it comes to stuff like this."

Sara left her parents' house and got in her car and just drove. A cold rain splatted on the soft roof of her convertible, and she drove and cried and glanced at the letter on the front seat beside her. She knew she had a lot of decisions to make.

The only peace that filled her came later, after she had read Ethan's letter yet again.

You helped change my life.

remembrances

ETHAN WALKED up to the small gravestone and laid a creamy white rose on the frozen blades of grass. The weather had turned bitterly cold, but so far no snow had fallen. Ethan wondered if the North Carolina mountains would get their usual helping of snow by Christmastime.

It had taken him a long time to get the nerve to come back to the cemetery close to the little church in Hartside, although he had passed it many times during the months he'd spent at the cabin. Now that he was here, all he could picture was the smiling face of his mother.

"Where are you?" he said aloud.

He wondered if her spirit was floating above him as he looked at her name on the stone. Or perhaps she stood beside him, holding his hand, telling him everything would be all right.

Will everything really be all right, Mom? he wondered. *Is everything going to turn out okay?*

In another day, Ethan would be on his way to Europe. This would be the last time he would visit his mother's grave for a while. *I hope I'm making the right decision.*

Ethan couldn't help believing that somewhere either close or far away, his mother could see him. That she knew about everything—how his life had changed, how he still loved a woman who was so close to getting married, how he had come once again to the mountains she had always loved. He wondered what she would tell him now. Probably something about how God has a purpose and everything works out for those who love him.

Her faith had never faltered, even through her illness. If only her son could be so strong.

Ethan knelt on one knee.

"Mom, I miss you," he said. "I wish you were still here. There are so many things I need help with, that I need to know about. I want to make up for lost time."

Images of his mother over the years passed through his mind. How can anyone ever replace the love they have for their mother? How can anyone ever try to fill the void a mother leaves behind?

He remembered one of his mother's last requests—to be buried in this cemetery next to Hartside Bible Church. Ethan still remembered almost every minute of the small funeral service. He had not been back here since then.

He stood and looked at the small church a short walk away. "God, I wish I understood why everyone I care about always leaves me," Ethan said. "I just want to know why. Can I know this one thing? Can I?"

The silent wind chilled him as Ethan walked back to his car. Perhaps some questions in life would simply never be answered.

I will never forget about you.

prayers

"HEAR MY PRAYER, heavenly Father. Please help me to know your will. I don't understand anything anymore—not my own heart, not my own actions. Everything I feel seems to contradict everything I do. Please help me know what to do, Lord. I want to do the right thing. I want to do what you want me to do."

Sara wiped the tears away from her eyes and looked up at the huge, glorious cross on the wall behind the church pulpit. She felt comfortable praying here in the empty sanctuary of her large church. This was the same church she would have been married in, the same church where she would have told Bruce how much she loved him and how she planned on spending the rest of her life with him.

Now she wondered if she would ever tell someone "I do." "Lord, please help me. Please give me peace. Please let me know what to do."

She knew what she wanted to do. Go find Ethan, tell him he's wrong about the wedding, tell him she still loved him, tell him everything could work out all right.

But would they be back at square one? Would he tell her once again that he still had no use for her God, the same God she prayed to now? that he hated God and blamed him for all his problems? What if it still boiled down to that one fact?

I won't cast you aside, Lord. You've allowed me to come this far. You've allowed this to happen. I won't dishonor your name.

Couldn't she make one exception? Couldn't she be with Ethan and hope that he would change one day?

What about Marietta Ware? a voice reminded her. *Remember what happened to her?*

But Sara needed to see Ethan. It had been so long. She needed closure. She needed to know what his earlier letter had said.

Sara thought of her mother again. The anger still boiled deep inside of her. Could she forgive her mother for hiding such an important letter from her? Would she ever know what that one letter her mother threw out had said?

"Lord, I know you promise us many things. You promised that you would send your own Son to die on a cross for all of us. You promise to take care of your children. I know you never fail to keep any of your promises. Yet why can't I have faith in that? Why can't I have any sort of strength now?

"Please, Lord, give me strength. Give me hope. Help me to forgive my mother when that's the very last thing I want to do. Give me strength, Lord. Give me your strength."

She looked up again at the cross.

"And Lord, if it be your will—only if it is your will—please let me find him one last time. I know it is selfish of me to ask. Maybe it would be better never to see him again. But please, Lord, please let me talk to Ethan one last time. I just need to know. I want to know if there is any hope of anything changing.

"More than anything, Lord, I want him to know you."

The doorbell brought Sara out of her trance as she sat in front of the television watching an uninteresting sitcom. So far,

TRAVIS THRASHER

it had not even made her smile. She looked at the digital clock on the VCR and knew it had to be her mother. No one else would stop by at nine-thirty at night to say hi.

Maybe it's Ethan. The thought popped into her mind before she could stop it. She just shook her head and looked out the window next to the front door. Lila Anthony was standing out there in the cold. Sara opened the door and let her mother in without saying anything.

"Brrr, it's getting colder outside," her mother said as if the argument earlier that day hadn't happened. Lila took off her coat. "Sara, can we talk?"

"I'm not in the mood."

"I need to explain some things to you."

"There's nothing to explain." Sara sat back down on the couch and acted as if she were watching the program. Her mother sat next to her. In her hands was an envelope.

"Sara, please. I'm sorry. I'm so sorry, honey. I didn't think any of this would happen. I was just trying to look out for you—"

"I told you, I don't need you looking out for me."

"I know. That's what your father said, too. He was pretty upset with me."

"I don't understand why you would do something like this," Sara said.

"Here. Just look at these. I'm not saying what I did wasn't wrong. I want you to know why I did it."

Sara took the two black-and-white photographs and examined them. She recognized her mother with her glossy dark hair and wide expressive eyes. But in the photo her mother was much younger—her hair long and straight, her face rounder and smooth. She had to be in her late teenage years.

"Who's this?" Sara asked. "It doesn't look like Dad."

In each photo, a boy Sara didn't recognize stood next to her mother. In one, he wore a football uniform and held on to his helmet with one hand and Lila's hand with the other. In the second photo, he had his arm draped around Lila. It was obvious he was quite tall and well built.

"That's Paul Thomas, the young man I was going to marry when I was a senior in high school."

Sara looked again at the photos. "What? You never told me about him."

"I was in love with Paul from years earlier, but he never noticed me until I was a senior. He was a football hero and all the girls loved him. He just happened to be crazy for me—once he noticed me, that is."

"Wait a minute," Sara said. "You started dating Dad shortly after high school, right?"

"Yes. Actually, right around the time of graduation."

"But you were going to marry this guy? Seriously?"

"Oh yes. He even proposed to me."

"Really? Why didn't you ever tell me about him?"

Lila forced a bittersweet smile to her face. Sara could still see the young beauty from years ago in the face she looked at now.

"He was part of me that I buried a long time ago, Sara. Paul Thomas was everything I had ever wanted. He was reckless and wild. He drank too much at parties and was always with some new girlfriend."

"Everything you ever wanted? Yeah, right."

"I'm serious. He was. He was good-looking and exciting, and I loved being around him. I figured I could marry him, and we would live happily ever after."

"What happened?"

"I found out he was sleeping with my best friend. He proposed to me before the end of our senior year, and then he broke my heart."

Sara looked at her mother and couldn't believe the words she was hearing.

"And Dad?"

"Your father was heaven-sent. He had always loved me, but it was after I broke up with Paul that I discovered just how much he cared. He was so tender and so patient. He helped me get over Paul, to realize Paul was all wrong for me. I finally realized that I was in love with your father."

The photos in Sara's hands seemed unreal. "Why didn't you ever tell me?"

"Paul died a few years after we graduated from high school. I had already married your father and had never heard from him again. I heard one day that he had been killed in a car accident. They said he had been driving drunk, and I wasn't really surprised. But a part of me died, too. I still loved him, Sara. I couldn't believe it, and I never would have admitted it to anyone. But I did still love him."

"I'm sorry, Mom."

Lila took her daughter's hand. "Sara, I never meant to hurt you. I have only wanted the best for you. From the very first time I heard you describe this Ethan Ware, all I could think about was Paul Thomas and how much he had hurt me. I didn't want that to happen to you."

"But Ethan's not like that, Mom."

"Maybe not. I don't know Ethan—you do. And besides, you're right—you're an adult. I just—I didn't want your heart broken. I always thought you'd find someone stable and successful like Bruce and you'd be happy."

"You and Dad are happy, right?" Sara asked.

The fine wrinkles under her mother's eyes moved as she smiled and nodded. "Of course we are. I've never once doubted he was the right one."

"I never thought there was anyone else besides Ethan. I just thought he'd forgotten about me."

"Sara, please forgive your meddling mother. I'm sorry for lying to you."

For the first time in years, Sara felt like a child again as she hugged her mother. They talked with each other for another two hours about love, loss, and life in general.

It was her mother's final comment that stuck with Sara. "Take your father's advice, Sara. Don't let anything interfere with your dreams. If you still love this Ethan, then do something about it."

I will always thank you.

questions

A PLEASANT AND WARMING FIRE crackled and lit the otherwise dark room. Ethan could hear the wind outside wailing into the night, confirming the newscaster's prediction about the winter storm. It had started two days ago, and it would still be pounding the North Carolina mountains for at least the next few days. Snow had already blanketed his car and the deck outside— so this Christmas Eve and tomorrow's Christmas Day would indeed be a white Christmas.

A lonely Christmas, too, Ethan noted. He would have been in Germany now, celebrating with his uncle's family. But flights out of the nearest airport in Asheville had been cancelled, and driving the distance to a larger airport was out of the question in this storm. His roofing buddy, Jeff, and his wife were out of town, visiting Jeff's sister in High Point. Even the Forrests, the elderly couple Ethan had come to know after fixing their roof, were away visiting relatives. So Ethan was alone.

He hadn't even bought a Christmas tree, but that was okay. Christmas wasn't about gifts and trees and all that other stuff anyway. He didn't need them to celebrate Christmas. And though it would have been nice to be with some family or friends, he could see that perhaps it was good to be alone. He had been alone for so long, and now he was about to leave and start a new life. Starting over was easier when you didn't have many attachments.

December 24. The date couldn't help but bring up thoughts of Sara. A day and a half from now, she would be getting married. It still amazed him that she had never responded to his letter from the spring. He wondered if she would reply to his latest letter.

Even if she didn't, Ethan was glad he had written them. And glad he had come to the mountains and ended up staying for so long. The last few months had left him refreshed and encouraged. He had been able to stay at his uncle's cabin, paying only for food, electricity, and water. He had made a little money doing odd jobs with Jeff, who had become a close friend. In his spare time, he wrote.

This was what life would be like if he was a full-time writer. What a great life that would be, too. Especially if he had someone to share that dream with.

Perhaps one day he would. But for now, he was alone in that dream—and he was surprised to find out that was all right.

In a sense, this past fall in the mountains had truly set him free. He was able to take walks in the high North Carolina hills with a notebook in hand and the entire universe seemingly at a standstill. Here, life didn't pass him by in a rush and a curse; here, one could breathe in life and the beauty of the earth. There were so many things he had grown up not appreciating—the blazing reds and sparkling golds of the autumn foliage, the nip in the air as winter approached, the comfort of a mug of canned soup sipped by the fire.

He found himself smiling every time he wielded the can opener, remembering the months when that had been all his mother could afford. Then, he had complained bitterly. Now, he relished the warmth of the memory.

TRAVIS THRASHER

That was something that had changed about him, he reflected. Now he appreciated so much more. For a while, he had almost given up on life. Now he was discovering, to his joy, that he valued life dearly.

Seeing Sara this past summer had been everything he wished it hadn't been. For weeks afterward, he had fought with himself about calling or writing or going to see her. He had kept on giving up on her, giving up on himself. But over time a strange thing happened. He had found his voice again. He had began to write—and now the words overflowed. Something was there. Something incredible. So he wrote and wrote and found that the same passion and the same yearning that had moved him as a young man was still very much there. If anything, it was stronger than it had ever been.

He had spent days reading and writing—enjoying the beauty around him and wandering the mountain roads looking for awe-inspiring views. His journals had filled with poetry and thoughts and love notes to Sara and dreams and desires. And then he had begun the novel, which only recently he had finished.

Perhaps this was the first big step in his life as a writer. He could already see the blurbs in the English-lit texts. Ethan Ware, after a difficult childhood full of loss and trauma, still loves his one and only childhood sweetheart, Sara. He discovers she is marrying another, so he goes to the log cabin to get away and in the course of the time there he begins to write—a little at first, then more and more, until he has penned his own Great American Novel. He goes to Europe and works some more on his writing, adding depth and resonance to his already distinctive voice. He gets his first book published, and, while it is not a huge success, it does start the career of perhaps the greatest living writer since Ernest Hemingway.

203≋ questions

I'm crazy, Ethan thought. *That's what Sara would tell me if she knew I was thinking like that. Crazy.* But she'd smile when she said it.

And the dedication page of his first novel, the first of many great works, would simply state the following:

"To Sara. The promise remains."

If he ever did publish anything, the dedication would read exactly like that. His promise still endured—even now, after realizing she was gone.

Ethan thought of his dreams and realized that for a while, they had left him. But he had been given the gift of his dreams again. He could dream as high as the heavens above. And if his great dream of a life with Sara Anthony was lost, there was still time for other dreams. Perhaps he would write and be famous, or perhaps he would remain an unknown dreamer all his life. And he was fine with that. He was willing to take what life brought him.

On this Christmas Eve, he sat reading a timeless classic, a book he had ignored during most of his youth. Now he simply sat back and thought about life. He remembered and felt a peace inside—a peace that felt soothing even though he had lost a love he would never forget.

He thought of his mother tonight and wished she were there to see him. He thought she would be happy—proud of the changes that had taken place in him. Perhaps she was looking down at him and smiling. She would always be with him, no matter where he went or what he did. She had guided him in the right direction, just as Sara had. The two most important women in his life had helped shape and direct him more than either knew.

TRAVIS THRASHER

But one day they would know. And one day they would receive their reward.

This Christmas Eve, as so many other families and friends and loved ones celebrated together, Ethan watched the fire burn low and thought once more of Sara. He missed her. And he still loved her. And he wondered if he would ever see her again.

The fire snapped back at him, and the winds outside hummed. Another noise, distant and strange, sounded. Something outside with the storm, that was all.

"Please let me see her again," he whispered, drifting in and out of sleep.

When the banging knock sounded, he thought a tree had fallen against the front door. But it wasn't a crash, because it continued, again and again. *Knock, knock, knock.*

Dressed in plaid pajama bottoms and an old but comfortable Washington Redskins sweatshirt, his hair long and falling in his eyes, the month-old thickness of beard on his face, Ethan stumbled to the door, wondering who it could be. Hopefully it wasn't some psycho looking for trouble on Christmas Eve.

The knocking continued.

He opened the door to the fury of wind and snow and saw outside a small figure bundled up with a hood and overcoat and boots. He could only see her dark, questioning eyes, but instantly he knew who it was.

Sara had found him.

Thank you for not giving up on me.

promises

ETHAN'S LETTER had started everything. But in the end, it had been the comment by Sara's mother that propelled Sara into action. "Take your father's advice, Sara. Don't let anything interfere with your dreams. If you still love this Ethan, then do something about it."

Sara still could not believe those words had come from her mother's lips. But they had, and they were all Sara needed to go and try to find Ethan, to at least see him one final time.

Sara called and tried to find a phone number for him. His Chicago number had been cut off. Trying to find a number for his uncle's residence in Germany was impossible. So she called other places, to no avail. Finally she decided to try her last hope—going to the little cabin in the mountains. That was where the letter had been sent from, so he obviously had been there not long ago. Probably he was long gone, but she had to try.

So Sara left on the morning of December 24, two days before a cancelled wedding date Ethan still thought existed. Her parents were not happy about her leaving a day before Christmas, and they were concerned about the most recent weather reports, but they understood she had to go.

Before she left, her father handed her a hastily wrapped Christmas present. "You can open the rest when you get back home," he said.

Sara opened the package and found a compass and a candy bar. "The compass is to help you find where you're going, and the Snickers is in case you get lost."

He smiled and kissed her on the cheek. Her mother was restraining herself, holding back both words and tears, but she managed a taut smile as well.

Sara hugged her mother. "Thank you, Mom."

That was all that needed to be said. They both understood what the thank-you was for. It had taken a lot out of Lila Anthony to give her daughter permission to follow a dream.

It didn't take long for Sara's convertible to make its way from Herrington Lane to Interstate 85. The radio made occasional references to the winter storm moving into the Smokies from the west, but she was pretty sure she could get through before conditions got really bad.

She had to get there.

During the entire trip in her car, she prayed. "Please, Lord, show me what to do. For months you've known my questions, my soul-searching. I believe this is what I need to do, what I have to do, but I need you to show me what your will is. Let me find Ethan—or at least find the truth. I need to know if there is hope for the two of us. But whatever happens between us, please let Ethan find your truth, Lord. That is what I have always prayed, and I know that you always have a plan and a purpose. I hope and pray that there is a plan and a purpose for Ethan and me."

Again and again, Sara found herself praying for guidance and direction and peace. And the trip went smoothly—up the interstate toward Greenville, South Carolina, and then back west toward Asheville, through the brightly decorated downtown, and then along the smaller highway that led into Hartside. But she got lost in the snow-covered hills as the storm she'd driven into halfway across North Carolina turned into a full-scale blizzard. She drove for two hours in the dark, suffocating snow, trying to find Chestwood Lane. She cried and tried to get a grip on herself. For a while she questioned the decision to come here. Not only was it foolish; it was dangerous.

Thank goodness she brought a cell phone as well as the candy bar. But whether her digital phone would find service this far out was an open question.

Suddenly it was there—Chestwood Lane. She felt like a small child finding her lost sled in a snowpile. Her car plowed through the thickening snow until she made it up the steep driveway.

It was already evening and the cabin, what little she could see of it in the cloudy storm, appeared dark. If she had come here for nothing—if he was gone and nobody was inside—she would not only feel stupid but be in a lot of trouble.

She would also be devastated.

Sara opened the car door and instantly felt the stinging bite of the storm. She was cold and stiff from the drive, and her feet slipped on the icy driveway as she started toward the house. She noticed something in the driveway covered with a thick blanket of snow—could it be a car? Ethan's car? Her heart beat faster as she approached the door. Closer to the small, lifeless cabin, Sara noticed no signs of habitation. The windows were coated with snow, the deck unshoveled, no footprints anywhere. The tang of woodsmoke in the air could easily come from one of the other cabins nearby.

Her heart sank to think she might have missed him. Nevertheless, she knocked and knocked on the heavy wooden door, hoping against hope somebody, anybody was there.

And then in a glorious answer to one of her many prayers, the door opened. Before her in the doorway stood the man of her dreams.

A stunned and weary Ethan Ware looked back at her in shock. For a minute, he didn't say anything and didn't move. He just stared blankly at her as if he was waking up from a long sleep. "Sara?" he finally asked, ushering her inside.

And before he could say anything else, before she could take off her coat or pull down her hood, Sara embraced the man she so dearly needed to see and hold. He hugged her back and they stood that way at the open doorway, with puffs of snow drifting inside.

They didn't care. For the moment, after so many years and so many words and so many memories and so many miles, they had found each other.

Sara sat on one of the two couches slanted in front of the fireplace. Ethan haphazardly threw some more big chunks of wood on the fire, apologizing for his lack of grace in maintaining the flames. Sara took off her coat and shivered, cold even in her jeans and sweater. Her frozen feet began to tingle as they warmed by the fire. She snuggled down into the big blanket Ethan had given her.

For a few minutes neither of them said much. Sara was cold and frightened and out of breath, so Ethan focused on getting her warm and relaxed. Outside the winds picked up and the snow continued to fall. His words came out awkward and forced, sounding strange in his ears.

Fixing her some hot tea took several minutes. He handed her the mug, then said, "Excuse me for a second."

He came back in jeans with his hair pushed back, a little neater. He sat on the couch across from her and smiled.

TRAVIS THRASHER

Sipping her tea and feeling warm and fairly sensible now, Sara looked hard at him. He was older, of course, and the beard wasn't a new thing. His blondish brown hair had grown long in front—the bangs fell down on his forehead—yet the back had been kept fairly short. He looked slim but healthy, his blue eyes glowing in the firelight. She stared and remembered—his eyes looked more captivating than she recalled. Something was different. The sadness that used to surround them no longer seemed to be there.

For a couple of minutes they only smiled at one another.

"I can't believe you're here," Ethan said.

"I can't either." Sara released a nervous laugh.

"Remember the last time you were here?" Ethan asked, smiling at her. "Seems like storms follow you."

"I was so afraid I wasn't going to find the cabin, that you weren't going to be here, that—" And the control she thought she had regained with the warmth and hot tea and the safety vanished. She began crying again.

Instantly Ethan was at her side, kneeling on the floor but not touching her. "It's okay. You're here. You made it. It's all right."

"Oh, Ethan, I don't know what to think or feel anymore. I just—don't—know." She continued to cry.

Ethan looked up at her and smiled. "You are so beautiful—you know that?"

"No, I'm not. I probably look terrible. I've been crying for the last day it seems. Make that the last six months."

Ethan looked at her and didn't say anything. He looked surprised by her comment. But then he smiled again and pointed to himself.

"I hope you know I sure wasn't expecting any company. Look at me. I'm like Grizzly Adams walking around here. My hair looks like it's out of some horror movie."

Sara looked at him and laughed. It felt good to hear jokes again. "It's good to see you," she said softly.

"I'd say the same thing, but that's quite an understatement," Ethan said, still kneeling beside her.

The fire and one other light were the only illumination in the room. Sara didn't mind. She only needed enough to look into Ethan's eyes.

"I got your letter a few days ago," Sara said. "I've tried to call, to get hold of you. I thought you had gone to Europe or somewhere and, well, I just panicked."

Ethan looked up, his face questioning. "Panicked?"

"Yes, I-I need to explain something to you. I need to tell you what happened."

"What do you mean? About getting engaged? I know about that."

Sara shook her head. "Ethan, I . . . I'm not engaged. Not anymore."

"You got married early?"

Sara couldn't help but smile as she answered his desperate reply. "I called it off."

The look on Ethan's face evolved in an everlasting minute. He looked elated and stunned and horrified all in one. He tried to say something but couldn't.

"I had to find you."

"When did you—you know?" Ethan asked.

"Back in July. After my trip to Hartside to find you."

"But you never found me."

"I know."

"Then why—"

She held up a hand to stop his words. "Let me explain. Please." Sara proceeded to tell him her story, to tell him words she knew he needed to hear.

TRAVIS THRASHER

She talked about Bruce, who he was and why she had started dating him. About being a schoolteacher and realizing she was thirty years old and not married, about her need to get on with her life. About Bruce's proposal and her halfhearted acceptance and about thinking she could learn to love Bruce, even though she still had all these feelings for Ethan.

As she spoke, Ethan's eyes began to fill with tears.

Sara continued, telling how she had returned to Hartside searching for an answer and realized she could not marry Bruce. She kept describing how she couldn't believe that he had not written or let her know how he was doing. She believed he had given up on her.

She saw the objection cross his face as she said it, and she held up a finger to silence him. Then she went on to tell about the past week, starting with the letter she had received and then the discovery that her mother had discarded the previous one.

"She what?" Ethan asked, stunned.

"My mom, she—I know, it's horrible. I'm so sorry. She didn't know what she was doing. I mean, she did, but now she's sorry. She is very sorry."

"The letter, my letter? She threw it away? Why?"

"She knew Bruce was going to propose to me. And she thinks Bruce is wonderful—he is, actually—and she wanted me to marry him. So then the letter came, and she just sort of panicked and hid it. Then she threw it out."

Ethan's face showed anger first, and Sara felt afraid he might say something bitter or cutting. But then his face changed. He glanced at the fire and then back at Sara. He burst out laughing. "You've got to be kidding."

"What?" Sara said, wiping tears out of her eyes.

"No, this is good. Actually, I think it's the best thing I've heard in a long time."

"What?" she repeated.

"Your mom. What she did, it was horrible, but—wow, am I relieved."

"You're relieved?" Sara asked. Now she was utterly confused.

"Yes. Tell me. Did your mom read the letter?"

"No, she just threw it out. I'm sorry."

Ethan stood up, moving over by the fire. He took the poker and stirred the coals. He was almost too excited to sit still. "No, no. It wasn't your fault. It wasn't at all your fault. That makes sense, I think. It's great." He laughed.

"What? What's so funny?"

"So you came up here on Christmas Eve to tell me all this?"

"Yes," Sara said. "And to find out about us. About you and me, I mean."

Ethan nodded and sat back down, this time beside her.

"The last time you were up at this cabin, all those years ago, you told me how sorry you were that we couldn't be together. You said you still loved me, but we couldn't be together. Has that changed?"

Sara wondered for a second. "No. I mean, the love and everything is still there, if that's what you mean. But, as far as the other—"

Ethan smiled and stood back up. "I've always dreamed of this. I've dreamed it for so long. I just didn't believe it could happen."

Then he disappeared. Sara felt unsure what his giddiness was about. She wanted to know about the letter, about whether there was any hope for them to be together.

Ethan came back with a piece of lined paper, crumpled and well worn. He sat back down beside her and smiled.

"You know, I've read this thing to myself a million times, I think, ever since I sent it. I just couldn't believe that you never responded or never said anything to me about it. I just couldn't understand why. But now—well, here you are."

"Is it a copy of the letter?" Sara asked.

"It was my first draft," he answered. "You know how we writers are, making sure we write the exact thing and get it right. So this one probably isn't as polished as the one I sent you, but all the thoughts are there."

"So can I read it?" Sara asked.

"Let me read it to you. I always wanted to tell this to you in person, but I hadn't seen you in so long that I wasn't sure how you felt about me."

So Ethan began to read the letter, sitting next to Sara in front of the roaring fireplace. Sara stared into his eyes, focusing on every word he uttered.

"My dearest Sara. Where can I begin? It has been a long time, too long, since you last heard from me. I am sorry for that, and I apologize for not writing to you sooner. Many things have happened to me and most of them, I believe, are because of you. For this I want to thank you.

"I also want you to know that I still think about you all the time. Every sunrise blossoms with the memory of you. All I have to do to see you again is close my eyes, and you're there. As much as I have traveled, trying to figure out why I can't write and why I can't even think straight, there has been one thing I can say with absolute confidence: I love you. I still dream of being with you.

"After my mom passed away, my whole world ended. I think you knew that. And you were there, as always, and I thought that if I could have you, if you could be mine, life would be okay again and I could get through anything. I believed I could find peace in you, the girl with a smile that could melt the coldest of hearts. So that day when you said goodbye to me at my uncle's little cabin, I felt I had experienced another death.

"I lost hope in everything. In every dream I ever had. In everything I had ever believed in. My writing stopped. My passion for life stopped. Everything stopped. And yet, I still continued to love you. You were all I could think of.

"I lost myself there for a while, wandering here and there and searching for something. But during that lost time I reread all your letters and tried to figure out what it was about this love of yours. Why was it different than mine? You loved me, yet you couldn't be with me—how absurd was that? But of course you had explained it before. You could not give yourself to somebody who didn't hold the same beliefs as you, couldn't share the same faith that kept you going. You couldn't do that to me or to yourself. You were unable to make that commitment—and you were right.

"Yet, at the same time, you loved me enough to never give up on me. I noticed in your letters the Bible quotes you would write and all the things you would say about them, and I usually passed them off as simply cute—like you. I understand now that you were trying to explain eternal things to me. I just never really listened."

Ethan stopped and looked up at Sara. "Are you okay? Do you really want to hear this?"

"No, no, I'm fine." Sara wiped her eyes and smiled. "Please, go on. I can't believe I almost never heard this."

"I always did want to read this to you myself," Ethan said. "Okay, where was I? Yeah, I just never listened.

"But then I started to listen, because there was nothing else to listen to. I had lost my family and you and my writing and everything that was important to me. So I started searching for something—I didn't even know what. I told myself that if believing in this God of yours could bring you back, I would do it. I would simply believe. But of course it wasn't as easy as that.

"I still had that little Bible you sent to me years ago. Remember? So I read it and read it and began to search myself and began actually to try to pray. And then I came across 1 Corinthians 13. The love chapter. I read it and reread it and reread it.

"I especially love the verse that says, 'There are three things that will endure—faith, hope, and love—and the greatest of these is love.' That's beautiful. I mean, it's not only great writing, which I can appreciate, but it says something beautiful about love.

"So I read more, trying to figure out why you loved me and yet didn't want to be with me. I read Matthew, Mark, Luke, and John. Verses stood out—like this one: 'Then Jesus told him, "You believe because you have seen me. Blessed are those who haven't seen me and believe anyway." '

"And then I came across that verse, the famous verse I have heard all my life but never understood: 'For God so loved the world that he gave his only Son, so that everyone who believes in him will not perish but have eternal life.'

"And I began to cry after reading that. I was at the lowest point I had ever reached. I felt totally alone, and I finally realized that nothing or no one could fill that emptiness. Only Christ could, this Jesus Christ I had heard about from my mom and from friends and from you—from sweet little Sara Anthony. From my love.

"So I finally prayed to Jesus not to help me find you but to help me find him. To forgive me for all my wretched sins and to give me some sort of peace. I needed help—not because I was so love stricken, but because I was lost and needed to open up to the truth I had been hearing all my life.

"And then, just like that, Christ answered. He gave me this

peace—it's hard to describe, but I know it's real. I guess you know what I mean.

"Sara, do you remember the promises we made so long ago? I promised I would never stop loving you, and you promised you would never stop praying for me. Well, I guess you kept your promise, because those prayers were answered, Sara. My mom's prayers were answered, too, bless her heart. I want—I need—you to know this.

"There aren't enough words to describe my love for you. But I can understand if what you felt and the love we shared has passed by. No matter what, I want you to know that your love has meant more to me this way than it ever would if you had stayed by my side. You loved me enough to say no to me, and your love gave me a chance to find Christ's love. Now I think I can actually begin to understand that love, the love God has for us.

"I still have so much to learn. There is still so much to comprehend. But as John said in his last words in his book, 'I suppose that if all the other things Jesus did were written down, the whole world could not contain the books.'

"I believe this is so very true. Perhaps one day my insignificant words could somehow, in some way, describe this amazing thing that Jesus did for me. Rescuing me from a lost life full of unhappiness. Filling me with hope and with a life. Giving me his promise of eternal life. He didn't have to pick me, Sara. But he used you to lead me to him. I thank him for that.

"I know the future is in God's hands, and I feel okay about that. I used to want to bargain with life, but I know I can't do that anymore. I'm curious, though. What about our promises? Have you forgotten? I'm not sure I'll ever know. But if I don't hear from you ever—here on earth, I mean—then I know I will still see you in the

TRAVIS THRASHER

future. I will see you and let you see the love you have allowed me to know. God's love.

"Thank you, Sara. Thank you for so much. Now I understand the things you once described for me. I pray to see you again, perhaps just for a moment. There are so many things I want to tell you.

"I won't dare ask again, but I still wonder what you will say when you read this. Am I simply being foolish to think so much about you? I don't know. So I'll just say goodbye again. But you need to remember these words. You need to know this, how much you helped change my life. I will never forget about you; I will always thank you. Thank you for not giving up on me.

"Sincerely, The starry-eyed dreamer you met years ago and never gave up on. Ethan."

Ethan put down the letter and smiled. He looked over at Sara, reached out a hand, and gently wiped away her tears.

"Well, that was it," he said.

Sara sat speechless, overcome by a joy that sent a thousand days and hours and lifetimes of worry away from her. She looked into the bright blue eyes of the man sitting next to her and realized it now, realized why something really was different about him. The boy she had fallen in love with had been a starry-eyed dreamer, a hopeless romantic, and the love of her life. She had loved the fun in his voice, the sparkle in his eyes. But he had grown cynical and skeptical about his own life, and a sadness had settled over him, a sadness she could even feel in his laughter. This sadness had only increased over the years, especially with the death of his mother.

Now that sadness had been replaced with a newfound love and a newfound faith. A faith in Christ. The sparkle had returned.

Sara threw her arms around Ethan and wept on his shoulder. This all felt like some wonderful dream—some incredible, awe-inspiring dream she could not have even imagined.

"I can't believe this," Sara said in Ethan's ear.

"It's true. It's all true. Everything."

"Ethan, I love you so much."

They continued to hold one another as the golden fire leaped in the background and the gentle shadows danced on the walls.

God grants to all of us moments in time like this, Sara thought. *Moments that we do not deserve, but moments we are given anyway.* This was one of the many gifts God had given to Sara and to Ethan. One of the countless many.

Thank you, Father. Thank you for letting me find him again. And thank you for letting him find you.

"Hold on," Sara said to Ethan. She stood up and went to her coat, which lay on the kitchen table only a few feet away from them.

"What?"

"I've got something to give to you," Sara said. She fished out a small object and carried it back to the couch. She slipped it in his hand as he had done so many years earlier to her. "Perhaps the timing on this wasn't exactly right," Sara said.

Ethan opened his hand and looked down at the small box. He grinned, and his hands shook. "You kept it?" he asked.

"Of course I did. Just like I kept my promise."

"Did you ever—"

"No," Sara answered back, knowing his question. She had never once opened it, not even to peek inside. She knew what was in there. She had never wanted to look at it, not without having Ethan at her side, not without the ability to tell him yes.

Ethan didn't hesitate. He opened the box and looked at the simple gold band with the tiny diamond. Then he got on one knee in front of her.

TRAVIS THRASHER

"I couldn't think of a better time to ask you, Ms. Sara Anthony, than on the eve of Christ's birthday."

Sara looked at the glistening ring she had waited and prayed for so long to see, to accept, to wear. Now. Finally, now. Thank God she had waited for his timing to be more than perfect.

"You waited for me, Sara," Ethan continued. "You waited and you kept your promise. And as crazy as I've been, I kept my promise, too—I've never stopped loving you. And now I think that I'm either going to run outside in the freezing cold and wake up and realize this is a dream or else do what I should have done years ago. The right way."

Ethan took Sara's trembling left hand in his own unsteady one. "Sara, will you do me the incredible honor of accepting my crazy and long-awaited and dearly meant proposal of marriage? Will you marry me?"

And Sara nodded, speechless. Love. Dear love. Dear heavenly love. She had waited and believed and now, could it be real? Could he really be standing in front of her slipping that beautiful diamond ring on her finger? Could he really be there, kissing her hand and holding it to his face to wipe away his own tears?

Could this be true, Lord? Please tell me it is.

"I do, I do—oh, I do," she said.

And then she held him once again in her arms. Outside, a storm howled, and the rest of the world seemed remote and cold and brutal and unrelenting. But inside the light was soft and warm and infinitely safe. The two of them had found each other. The promise had indeed remained, after all these years.

When Sara finally spoke again, she said these words to Ethan. "Thank you," she whispered.

He chuckled, not understanding her words. "Why thank me?"

"For never giving up on me, even after all these years and even after finding out I was engaged. Thank you."

"I would have always loved you, Sara. Even if you got married and went off and spent a lifetime with somebody else you dearly loved. God allowed you to come across my path. He allowed you to inspire me. And he helped you point me in the right direction. How could I not love you, no matter what?"

Ethan pushed himself to his feet, then sat down next to her. She nestled up close beside him.

"The storm looks bad, doesn't it," she said, looking through the frosted window at the cold and dark world. "And it's only going to get worse, I think."

The man she loved, the man who had waited so long for her and had found his way in this cold and dark world, reflected on her words.

"We'll make it," Ethan replied. "By God's grace, we'll make it. We've come this far, right?"

The fire continued to burn and the winds continued to howl and the snow continued to fall.

And the promises two young and loving individuals had made to one another on another storm-filled day still held true. As would the promises of the one who had brought them together, for an eternity.

Sincerely,
The starry-eyed dreamer
you met years ago
and never gave up on.

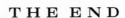

THE END

ABOUT THE AUTHOR

Travis Thrasher spent his youth living with his
family in places such as Australia, Germany, Florida,
and New York state. The longest period of time was
spent in the beautiful hills of western North Carolina,
where *The Promise Remains,* his first novel, is set. He
lives with his wife, Sharon, in suburban Chicagoland.

Travis welcomes letters written to him in care
of Tyndale House Author Relations, P.O. Box 80,
Wheaton, IL 60189-0080.